Contra Mundum Press

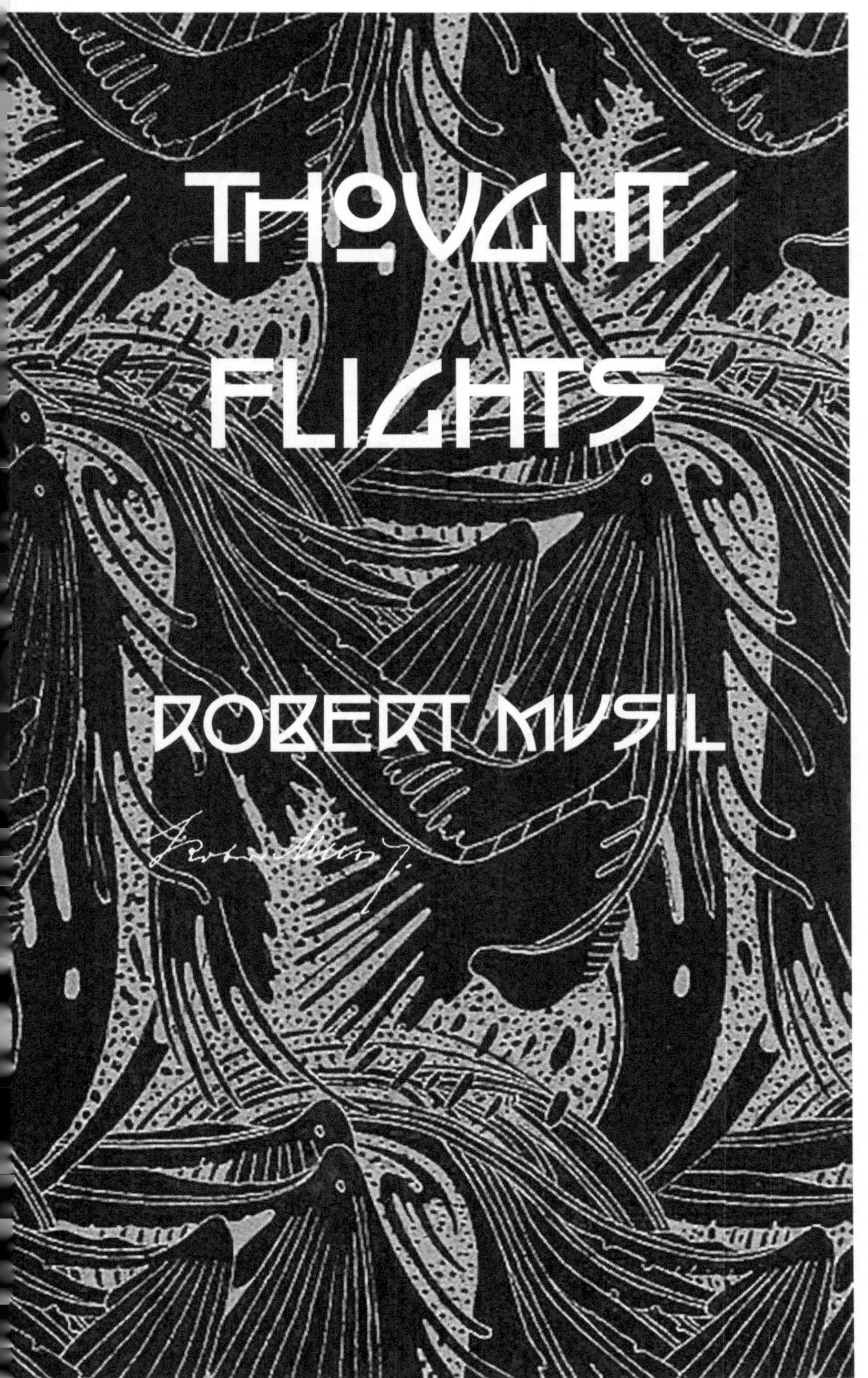
THOUGHT
FLIGHTS
ROBERT MUSIL

Selected Other Works by

Robert Musil in English Translation

The Confusions of Young Törleß

Diaries

The Enthusiasts

Five Women

The Man without Qualities

Posthumous Papers of a Living Author

Precision and Soul: Essays and Addresses

Vinzenz and the Mistress of Important Men

THOUGHT FLIGHTS

ROBERT MUSIL

TRANSLATED WITH AN INTRODUCTION BY GENESE GRILL

Contra Mundum Press New York · London · Melbourne

First Contra Mundum Press edition 2015. This edition of *Thought Flights* is based on the 2009 edition of the *Klagenfurter Ausgabe*

Library of Congress Cataloguing-in-Publication Data

Musil, Robert, 1880–1942

[Selections from Die Klagenfurter Ausgabe. English.]

Die Klagenfurter Ausgabe / Robert Musil; translated from the original German by Genese Grill

—1st Contra Mundum Press Edition

348 pp., 5×8 in.

ISBN 9781940625102

I. Musil, Robert
II. Title.
III. Grill, Genese.
IV. Translator & Introduction.

2015936820

CONTRA MUNDUM PRESS gratefully acknowledges the financial support received for this translation from the AUSTRIAN MINISTRY OF EDUCATION, ARTS, & CULTURE.

TABLE OF CONTENTS

III. LITERARY FRAGMENTS

IV. UNPUBLISHED GLOSSES

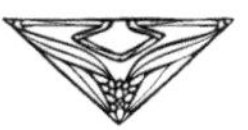

INTRODUCTION

I. THOUGHT FLIGHTS

> *My thoughts were soon crippled if I tried to force them in any single direction against their natural inclination — and this was, of course, connected to the very nature of the investigation. For this compels us to travel over a wide field of thought crisscrossing in every direction... The same or almost the same points were always being approached afresh from different directions, and new sketches made...*
>
> —Wittgenstein, *Philosophical Investigations*

An expert legal counselor in Robert Musil's "The Fairy Tale of the Tailor" accuses the tailor of suffering from "thought flight": "He cannot remember what others have told him a hundred times already; instead he is always looking for new ideas" (25). Insofar as new ideas are anathema to the preservation of the status quo, thought flight may be seen by some to be an anti-social disease that breeds art. For Musil, & for his one-time neighbor Ludwig Wittgenstein, art is a special mode of expression that resists ossification and false deductive reasoning by specializing in the particular case presented in *living* words. It is a "conduct of life in examples," whose form & content can not be categorized into clichés.

The tension between clichéd categorization, more meaningful abstraction, and the proliferation of particular or partial cases constitutes one of Musil's central concerns in these small prose pieces. His experimental use of language is an object lesson in how a creative use of the shared store of used and even abused words can explode standardization and ossification. As a master of unexpected metaphor and surprising analogy, Musil vividly enacts in these pieces a strategy for both illuminating & ameliorating the crisis of language that haunted his contemporaries.

As always, Musil is really asking: how shall we live? And how can an artistic, experimental method of looking at the world help us to keep the debasement of language and the advent of deadening standardization at bay? How can we resist succumbing to that "stereotyped world" of theory and habit that Walter Pater already warned against in his conclusion to *Studies in the History of the Renaissance*? Today, in a time of pervasive standardization of thoughts, objects, and persons, an age wherein language is deteriorating into a handful of utilitarian abbreviations, an age of globalization, homogeneity, & the reduction of almost everything to the lowest common denominator, Musil's defense of the individual, of the idiosyncratic, & of the free thought, word, or act, his often hilariously ironic — but quite serious — treatment of the "age of money," simulation, & sameness, is now more trenchant than ever, and equally if not more pertinent. While Musil vividly evokes the secrets and scandals of cosmopolitan Vienna and Berlin in the 20s & 30s, reacting with wit and wisdom to innovations in technology, art, and politics in his glosses, and exploring the psyches & lives of himself and his contemporaries in his stories and literary sketches, we cannot help but recognize in them our own time and troubles.

It is Musil's special genius to be able to move effortlessly from discussing fashion to the Kantian categorical imperative, and to write with humor, lyricism, and fervor in an open genre availing itself of poetic prose, philosophical essay, fictional narrative, and feuilletonistic lightness. He writes about suit styles, political corruption, social conformity, morality, industrial standardization, language, technology, the legal system, his childhood memories, love, modern art and the destruction of nature; but he is simultaneously asking exacting philosophical questions about the relationship between recurring abstractions and particular facts. He strenuously advocates for the individual, the exceptional, the empirical and experimental mode of *what is*, without ever fully relinquishing the uses of abstraction, idealism, or the importance of imagining *what could be*. Because for Musil, a self-styled "*Monsieur le Vivisecteur*," it is, to borrow Pater's words, "only the roughness of the eye that makes any two persons, things, situations seem alike."[1]

1. Walter Pater, *Studies in the History of the Renaissance* (London: Macmillan & Company, 1873) 211.

The real is variegated, changeable, irreducible. And art — as opposed to science or abstract philosophy — can readily figure forth that differentiation. Yet again, art and language do require some level of abstraction, some commonalities, and some concessions to metaphoric similarity. And metaphor brings, in Musil's words, "beauty & excitement" into the world.[2] And when two usually separate things unite, thoughts "fly."

II. SELECTION & ARRANGEMENT

The texts in this volume have been selected by myself out of a mass of *Nachlaß* material (literary remains) and collected under the title *Thought Flights*. Despite the fact that Musil jokes in the introduction to his own collection, *Posthumous Papers of a Living Author*, that he does not usually approve of posthumous publications, we also know that he tried very hard amid the fascist atmosphere of the 1930s, as the publication of his continuing work-in-progress on the novel became increasingly improbable, to make arrangements for the publication

2. Robert Musil, *The Man without Qualities*, Vol. I, tr. by Sophie Wilkins, ed. by Burton Pike (New York: Knopf, 1995) 625.

of many unpublished small prose pieces and aphorisms abroad, hoping to have them translated into English & French, but mostly to no avail.[3]

It is a daunting responsibility to select which pieces of Musil's voluminous *Nachlaß* to present to an English-speaking public that has little to no idea of the mass or content of the existing texts. There are myriad fragments, in diary entries & in folders arranged by Musil, with complex numbering and cross-referencing systems, arranged by theme, character, plot line, possible project. One such folder is titled suggestively, "Beginnings and Notes"; another, revealing our author's ambitions beyond *The Man without Qualities,* is called "The Twenty Works." While one may naturally be eager to access this *Nachlaß* in its entirety, some method of selection is called for, whereby one judiciously ascertains which texts warrant being shared first, and in what context.

3. See Gunther Martens, "Robert Musils Kurzgeschichten: an den Rand geschrieben?" [Robert Musil's Short Stories: Written in the Margins?] *Mitteilungen des Deutschen Germanistenverbandes,* 61.2 (2009) 246–257. "For Musil, the short prose only became relevant again when, after 1933, the possibility of even publishing the remaining part of the still unfinished novel *The Man without Qualities* became increasingly unlikely. In letters Musil mentioned more than once the consideration of publishing "'short prose works & aphoristic reflections' (in the format of N[ietzsche] or V[aléry] for example)" (248).

Thus I have been fortunate to have the guidance of Walter Fanta, an expert in the genealogy of Musil's texts, and the chief editor of the *Klagenfurter Ausgabe* (the edition from which I have taken these pieces), in making the selections. All of the small prose pieces that we can reliably attribute to Musil, ones that he published in journals, newspapers, and magazines during his lifetime but did not include in his *Posthumous Papers of a Living Author*, are included here in sections one and two ("Stories," "Glosses").[4] The latter two sections of this book ("Literary Fragments" and "Unpublished Glosses") contain unfinished pieces, selected among many on the basis of a few simple criteria, mainly a matter of genre & level of completion. While there are numerous short drafts of similar length in Musil's *Nachlaß*,

4. This excludes the many pieces written during World War I for the Tirolian *Soldatenzeitung* (Soldier Newspaper) that Musil edited, which are mostly unsigned and still require editing before definitive attributions can be made to them. One slightly controversial piece, "The Twilight of War" (not written for the war paper, but published rather in the journal *Roland* on January 1, 1925), has been included in this volume although at least one scholar seems to think it may not have been written by Musil since it is not signed and is the only published piece of Musil's writing that directly argues against war. Others, like Walter Fanta, see it as self-evident that Musil wrote this piece and deliberately did not sign it because of his professional affiliation with the Austrian army.

many of them were conceived as parts of the project that eventually became *The Man without Qualities* (fragments under the titles "Grey-Eyes," "The Archivist," "The Twin Sister," et cetera), while others were conceived as, or later developed into, entirely separate novel-length projects (such as the fascinating notes for Musil's utopian fantasy *The Land over the South Pole*, otherwise known as *Planet Ed* or *The Contemporaries*). Some fragments that seem to have been intended as small prose pieces have not been included because they are only a few sentences long, are mixed in with notes for other projects, or are too sketchy to provide a clear idea of Musil's vision. Others have not yet been definitively attributed, or the manuscripts from which they have been transcribed are still being edited. For this volume, then, I have chosen to include works that have attained a certain level of finish, that are ascertained to be definitively his, and that generally fall within the genre called "small prose."

But what is "small prose" and why did an author consumed with a large unfinished (and possibly unfinishable) project take the time to write it? Many of Musil's contemporaries wrote brief, often light, discursive, observational pieces for newspapers and journals, mixing autobiography, prose poem, philosophical commentary, social critique, fairy tale, lyricism, parable and humorous squib, and often collected them into books. While some of these authors are still known today, others have been largely forgotten, at least in the English-speaking world.

A brief who's who of the world of Germanic small prose would include Robert Walser, Alfred Polgar, Franz Kafka, Peter Altenberg, Walter Benjamin, Karl Kraus, Jan Neruda, Egon Erwin Kirsch, Siegfried Kracauer, inter alia. That many writers, including Musil, wrote brief *feuilleton* pieces, or "glosses," for newspapers in order to make money certainly played a role in the proliferation and establishment of the genre,[5] but brevity, speed, lightness, sketchiness, freshness, and the agility necessary to quickly shift perspectives or relative stances were also generally valued qualities of the day.[6] In an imagined interview with Alfred Polgar, whose book of small prose

5. See Gunther Martens: "Robert Musils Kurzgeschichten: 'An den Rand geschrieben'?" where he notes that authors of the time, including Musil, wrote to fit the constraints of the *feuilletons*, the length & the "casual improvised" nature. Authors used these constraints to develop "a unique form of self-referentiality & multi-level coding" (246).

6. See "'Stoffe sehr verschiedener Art... im Spiel... in eine neue, sprunghafte Beziehung zueinander setzen': Komplexität als historische Textur in Kleiner Prose der synthetischen Moderne" ["'Putting material of very different sorts... in play... in a new, mercurial relationship to each other': Complexity as Historical Texture in Small Prose of Synthetic Modernism"] in Thomas Althaus, Wolfgang Bunzel, & Dirk Göttsche (eds), *Kleine Prosa: Theorie und Geschichte eines Textfeldes im Literatursystem der Moderne* [Small Prose: Theory and History of a Textual Field in the Literary System of Modernism] (Tübingen: Niemeyer, 2007) 254–279. Small

Written in the Margins he celebrated, Musil writes that, "The literature of the future will have something of newspaper prose about it, not its false ethos, but its prosaic prose."[7] And this prose will, despite the shortcomings of newspapers, have the energy of a "volcano from which the times spews its fermentation," or the complexity of the "unceasing ringing of contradictions in all telephones." It will, like Musil's own prose, avail itself of Polgar's subtle technique of "simultaneity," whereby he presents "things that go together in life but really cannot abide each other as soon as the atmospheric sauce of habit is removed," or it will echo Polgar's tendency

---

prose is defined by Frank & Scherer as a form characterized by "unfinished combinations, small models of alternate perspective, of sensory perception & an intellectual synthesis of empirical phenomena, which avails itself of the knowledge of as many disciplines as possible — delivered in a prose form that is manageable, one that no longer explicates but rather condenses lyricism, narration, and reflection into literary images" (254).

7. *Klagenfurter Ausgabe* [Klagenfurt Edition]: *Annotated Digital Edition of the Collected Works, Literary and Biographical Remains, with Transcriptions & Facsimiles of All Manuscripts*, edited by Walter Fanta, Klaus Amann, and Karl Corino (Klagenfurt, Austria: Robert Musil Institute, Alpen-Adria Universität, 2009). From now on *KA. Transkriptionen und Faksimiles. Nachlaß Mappen. Weitere Mappen. Abschriften aus Essays/162. (Literaturheft № 10. März 1926. Interview mit Alfred Polgar von Robert Musil.)*

of "letting things that he wants to criticize promenade guilelessly about in the middle of the most praiseworthy impressions."[8]

In a piece included in this collection, Musil's "P.A. & the Dancer," Peter Altenberg, that famous Viennese café flâneur and feuilletonist, is depicted as a "beloved author" who walks tirelessly along the edge of a mountain, sweetly and sadly, ever retreating into the distance as the times rush on away from him: "He heals the soul with a hundred genuflections and the body with encouragements; he calls this awakening the life energies. He is at his best when he is laughed at" (165). The writer as half fool, as observer on the margins, as a tender motile eye looking at a world that is constantly shifting too.[9] While it may seem strange to suggest that Musil, who was actually accused of being "too intelligent to be a creative writer," might associate himself with foolishness, his "On Stupidity" essay makes a good case for both the æsthetic & ethical uses of being a fool in the eyes of the world; and in an early version of material that would make its way into *The Man without Qualities*, he imagines his protagonist Ulrich as a "Hans Narr," a German version of our proverbial Jack the Knave.[10]

8. *KA: Interview mit Alfred Polgar.*

9. Gunther Martens notes that Musil's "essayistic small prose" foregrounded "self-reflexively, the conditions of observations" (255).

Musil once revealed something about his own working methods in a double review of Robert Walser's *Geschichten* (Stories) and Franz Kafka's *Betrachtungen* (Observations) written in 1914 for *Der Neue Rundschau.*[11] Walser is depicted in the review almost like Musil's own tailor who suffers from thought flights. Musil imagines Walser on trial before a readership that finds him to be lacking in moral seriousness because he does not seem to have the expected reactions to either bad or good events (theater fires or nature walks). Musil ends by admitting that Walser's pieces are "Spielerei" (capers, shenanigans); and yet they are not merely *literary,* but rather human "Spielerei," "with much softness, dreaminess, freedom, and the moral richness of one of those seemingly unprofitable, lazy days, where our most settled convictions dissolve into a pleasant languorousness." Musil continues by telling us that although Walser's

10. See Musil's notes for an early version of the novel titled "House with No Other Side of the Street": "II. Version: The Foolish Hans who has come to an awareness of the uniqueness of his powers. The Foolish Hans who has cultivated his intellect. He searches for his sister — the one who was engaged, engaged late in life, and convinces her." *KA. Lesetexte. Band 4, Der Mann ohne Eigenschaften. Die Vorstufen. Aus dem Nachlaß Ediertes. Vorarbeit zum Roman. Haus ohne Gegenüber.*

11. *KA. Lesetexte. Band 13. Kritiken. Buchrezensionen. Literaturische Chronik* (Berlin: Der Neue Rundschau, 1914).

style is too unique to become its own genre, Kafka's first book, *Observations* (1913), seems (even though it appeared before Walser's book) like a special case of the Walser type:

> Here too, contemplation of a kind for which a writer fifty years ago would have invented the title Soap Bubbles; it suffices to note the specific difference and to say that here the same kind of invention has a sad tone while it is merry in the other, that there we have something freshly baroque, while here we have, in purposeful page-filling sentences, rather something of the conscientious melancholy with which an ice skater performs his long sweeps & figures. Very great artistic mastery here as well, but perhaps only an echo of those small endless paths into emptiness, a humble deliberate nothingness, a friendly tenderness of the kind that prevails for the suicide in the hours between decision and act, or however one will name this feeling which one could name in so many ways, because it simply resonates like a very soft dark middling tone.

It seems likely that Musil wrote his own small prose pieces as a distraction from his more strenuous work on his novel, and thus possibly considered them "Spielerei" too — but not merely of the literary kind; rather, human and morally rich, like Walser's; avoiding, also, expected uses of words and expected convictions; and conscientiously melancholy, endlessly expanding within the sort of mystical states Musil called "the other condition," timeless states hovering between decision and act, like Kafka's. Serious matters can be explored within seemingly light, frivolous frames and forms, large matters within short texts; whispers can carry weighty portent. Nothing is quite what we would expect; & above all we must guard against putting something entirely new into an old category. A "Spielerei" can be the perfect medium for turning an old certainty on its head, inciting profound insights, or making light of something all too ponderous or ossified.

Musil tells us something more about his approach to his small prose pieces in a December 8, 1924 letter to his friend Franz Blei, who had solicited a short piece for his journal:

> As I laid this letter aside yesterday as too gloomy, something came to me that I noted down. A little travel sketch with the code word coquetry; overnight it turned into a scheme. It is not at all original and is called "Susanna's Letter" because I turn the thing on its head and see it from the woman's perspective. In a few days you will receive it and more can come after. You'll have to take the lack of originality that comes with the letter form & with the disguise as a woman in stride if

> the rest of it is good; for this masquerade is personally fun for me, & my mood is in need of such a stimulus, even if it is a somewhat cheap one; on the other hand, the extraterritoriality of the woman in the world of men is an easy standpoint from which everything that one wants to discuss can be expressed in the same tone. This time it is only a little gossip within the realm of flirting, but the next time, or soon after, something else could follow... I don't want to sign these letters as Musil, but rather as Rychtarschow [Matthias Rychtarschow, a pseudonym Musil occasionally used, constructed from his paternal grandfather's first name and birthplace in Moravia], since I have not written anything serious for too long; in this way I do away with inhibitions which would otherwise certainly restrict me.

Within the pieces collected here, the reader will note repeating concerns and references, "Stichworte" (key words) which open up doors leading through the labyrinthine hallways of Musil's mind & meet up again in unexpected places. And these "Stichworte" run through all of Musil's work, and recur over and over again, as abbreviations and variations in notebook entries and drafts of essays, aphorisms, stories and novel chapters. As such, almost any genre of writing would serve just as well to explore whatever question exercised our author, seeming to invert Musil's commitment to the particular case. In fact, Musil once noted that the story of his twentieth-century siblings Ulrich & Agathe would have been "more impressive told as a story about Abdul Hasan Summum and Sufism."[12] In this instance, the general theme is more central than the particular iteration of the individual case, and may be represented or explored via a number of disparate examples. Theme then becomes particular case, and particular case becomes theme. The space between ideal and real, archetype and example, shrinks and expands amid myriad possibilities the way a living breathing person in a Walser story can suddenly become merely a pencil caricature on a café napkin (and vice versa). Musil wrote of his own working method:

> There are writers who are obsessed with one theme. They feel: this one or none at all; it's like love at first sight. The relationship of R[obert] M[usil] to his themes is a hesitant one. He has many at once and keeps them after the hours of first love are over, or even if there never were any such hours. He exchanges parts of them arbitrarily. Many half-developed themes wander and never surface in any book.[13]

---

12. Translated & included by Burton Pike in the *Nachlaß* section of *The Man without Qualities, Vol. II* (New York: Knopf, 1995) 1770.

13. *KA: Lesetexte. Band 14: Gedichte, Aphorismen, Selbstkommentare. Selbstkommentare aus dem Nachlass. Zum Roman Parerga und Paralipomena 1921–1937. Vermächtnis.*

So perhaps these small prose pieces can be considered occasional paramours to the great life-time love of the novel. The lover-author is still Robert Musil, with all of his neuroses, genius, obsessions, skills and fantasies, but without the devotion, frustration, profundity, ambivalent tenderness and habitual irritation of a long-term romance. In German an adulterous affair is called a *Seitensprung* — a side spring — which, perhaps, is not much different than a thought flight.

III. TRANSLATION CHALLENGES

Translating Robert Musil can be difficult for a number of reasons, all related to his original cast of mind. The first challenge is in allowing for his tendency to use unexpected words in unexpected combinations and to mix attitudes & qualities that would normally be considered to be in opposition if not even oxymoronic. So much communication consists in surmising *beforehand* what someone will say, inasmuch as people so often speak tautologically. With Musil we must always be on our guard against assuming or expecting anything. The writing and thought are devoid of clichés, and a translator must ever labor to resist choosing conventional phrases for original words and their syntheses. Within these pages, a motherly woman slices open a fish in her hand; torment is part of the pleasure of a day; an arrested man thinks his sentence is too short; domestic objects are sitting "in slippers, making faces" (40); a house burning down is an "insignificant occurrence" (52–53); an older woman's wrinkles are compared to the beautiful filigree work of a grand cathedral. We are always being asked to see conventional objects or situations in wholly new ways.

Another challenge for a translator is Musil's constitutional resistance to positioning himself securely on any specific side — a practice he may have learned from Nietzsche and which he praised in Polgar. Even when, as is often the case, he is criticizing or ridiculing some idea, some person, some situation, he is still often able to find something positive or useful or praiseworthy in what he is attacking. And while sometimes this positive valuation is meant ironically, sometimes it is not. About his resistance to taking definitive positions, in *Robert Musil: Literature and Politics*, Klaus Amann writes: "Musil's judgments are logical consequences of his [...] unbiased exploration of positions, stances, and situations. They are markers, stations, partial solutions of an ongoing, dynamic process of thinking."[14]

14. Klaus Amann, *Robert Musil: Literatur und Politik* (Reinbek: Rowohlt Taschenbuch Verlag, 2007) 31.

Amann then quotes a diary entry of Musil's explaining this speculative method of his:

> In the way that a bad person is a more daring speculator when he uses someone else's money than he is when spending his own, I want to follow my thinking out beyond the border of those things that, whatever the circumstances, I could justify; that is what I call "essay," "trial" (*D* 310–11).

Finally, Amann notes that

> Musil, in keeping with what he himself characterized as an 'intelligence that moves in different directions that contradict each other' (*D* 485), was rarely content with a position once it had been formulated. His impetus is doubt and his sword is the question mark, and that means constant revision & beginning anew.[15]

Musil's resistance to any fixed standpoint as well as his subtle irony is a challenge for a translator and the reader alike. Sometimes he will present an idea so far-fetched as to initially obstruct understanding. The reader (as the translator had before) will think that there must be a word missing, because he cannot possibly mean *that*. But if we unmoor ourselves from expected & conventional

15. Amann, *Literatur und Politik*, 32.

ways of thinking (in fact, only if we do so), we find something new. Thus, in "Moral Institutions" (88–92), we are told that *not* being prosecuted for a crime is worse than being prosecuted, because a prosecution at least confers a public character on a person, which is better than existing in moral limbo. Or in "An Example" (102–104), we are assured that if a questionable idea were to be manifested in reality it might in fact be favorable, since envisioned reforms always turn out much differently than was intended; and in one of the "Susanna Letters" (10–14), we are told that morality does more harm in the world than immorality. And these paradoxes compel us to resist the uncritical acceptance of commonplaces, assumptions, or facile solutions to complex problems.

Another translation challenge is Musil's specific attention to language & word usage. While in one gloss he writes that "a good writer will always understand how to write so that one could rearrange all of his words and even replace them with others, without changing the meaning" (130), this moment of reprieve for a lazy (but shocked) translator is immediately pulled out from under her feet by the ironic rejoinder: "this makes observation easy and corresponds to the modern principle of producing replacement parts that are readily available everywhere" (130). With Musil, every word is deliberate, and in some cases, of course, there is no correspondingly appropriate English choice. On the other hand, English often offers more word choices than German, & where

Musil thus sometimes is forced to repeat the same word within a few sentences, to keep slavishly to the narrower German possibilities can seem flat in English where we expect more variety. Of course, in instances where a repeated word seemed to me significant for the rhythm or meaning of a sentence, I have labored to maintain Musil's usage.

Where Musil's prose is remarkably buoyant in the original German, moving in a light and effervescent tempo over vast expanses of thought and reference, to reproduce this precarious balance between rhythm, lucidity, precision, and literary fluidity in English has naturally required some changes in syntax (particularly regarding sentence length) & word choice. What must be avoided at all costs in translating Musil is a mindless use of those "replacement parts that are readily available everywhere" — standardization — of language, metaphor, or syntax. Puns, of course, are problematic for all translators, and Musil's writing is no exception. I have tried wherever possible to create corresponding formulations, and where I could find no reasonable approximation in English, I have settled on a note explaining the richness lost in translation.

Translation of the unfinished texts posed its own problems, including the deciphering of abbreviations, gaps, repetitions, variations, and the possibility that Musil had not yet arrived at the right word or had inadvertently used the wrong word in a text that would have been corrected in a later revision. I have tried to move as gingerly as possible amid the unfinished possibilities, leaving most variations and repetitions, and choosing to present the reader with the rare opportunity of seeing Musil in the process of thinking and arranging, in reaching and fumbling for and alighting upon the right word. But in some cases I have removed a phrase or short paragraph that seemed too unfruitfully repetitive or too irrelevant to the piece, in which cases I have inserted ellipses in brackets and added an occasional note explaining what was deleted. In the case of abbreviations, I have tried to provide careful hypotheses where it was possible, but not to overreach in cases of uncertainty. In one instance (the very last piece in this volume, "Gœthe Year"), I have added a few stanzas of a Gœthe poem where Musil had only written the first line, assuming that he either would have taken the time to write it all out in the final version, or that his readers would be more familiar with the remainder than English-speakers today. Notes are likewise provided throughout to provide context that may have been lost over time and distance. But I have restrained myself as much as I could from adding too much scholarly commentary in the interest of the literary experience. May it be as fresh as possible. May it allow minds to open and be receptive to flying thoughts.

— Genese Grill, New Year's Day, 2015
Burlington, Vermont

I.

STORIES

SUSANNA'S LETTER

My Dear — I absolutely recommend that young men who have the looks for it bandage up one of their eyes; even in love less is more. On our last journey a man with only one eye sat across from me; the other was covered by a black bandage. I assure you, it is melancholy, this black-covered, dashing eye, withdrawn from the world; you can tell yourself ten times over that this man probably just poked his eye with his dirty fingers, but your fantasy doesn't want to believe that it is just a catarrh. You can also try to convince yourself as much as you want (if this one-eyed state really *did* have a poetic cause), that the poetry of having one eye, from Wotan to Wagner, is merely the kitsch of our brothers' dueling. Or that it is a handy excuse for husbands who, as soon as they attain the majestic years & begin to get comfortable, commonly point to Odin's example, whose wisdom was won at the expense of sensuality. It won't help you at all; the dark eye plays Chopin upon you.

You are more learned than I am: I think something like this is called a minus variant. It is a defect when looked at rationally, but it is arousing. That's how it was with me. The invention of the monocle certainly stems from this one-eyed business.

From this I gather what kind the pleasures of our times are: while the black-bandaged eye enhances the free one and renders it pictorially mysterious — one immediately searches for the other one — the "armored" eye smites its twin from the field. In fact I can't remember the eye color of a single one of our monocle-wearing acquaintances. And this is probably just the way they want it: glittering, dazzling, stabbing, but not allowing anyone to stab back. They have turned a spiritual attraction into a ridiculous intimidation technique. But I was able to discover the eye-color of my stranger right away. If it is true that a coarse log calls for a coarse axe, then, judging by the "sharpness" of this axe, our female fantasies today must really be first-rate German oaks.

The healthy eye of my stranger lay half in the shadow of his fur coat, hanging down from above. It appeared in response to a small movement whenever it wanted to look at me, which happened often enough. But as soon as I looked up, it disappeared just as adroitly. And the black oval of the bandage caught my look like a shield, while the receding enemy took aim from out of the jungle of the fur. On train rides that are not so long, this is quite a droll game. We both remained, as is only proper, fully earnest throughout. I know exactly what I look like. Not so young anymore, as you will admit. My chin was once energetic, and my neck straight. Today there is a light layer of fat over both, like a softly nestling scarf. Sometimes in the mirror this has an attraction for me, somewhat like the feeling of heavy winter garments. Or like longer clothes with high buttoned collars, under which the body can still just be sensed, aroused to the faintest state of excitement. The sort of excitement that arises from all kinds of uncertainty. I also love it that my hips, in contrast to my height, have just reached the extreme of width that is still beautiful, that the spindle of my thigh is still spun somewhat high, but not as high as it once was, and that I can no longer place a silk thread in the tender recess between my breasts and abdomen while standing up without having it fall down, as I once could. I think to myself, this is how an acrobat must feel on the tightrope in the lowest, most swaying middle. It is all downward going from here on out, but every step becomes calmer and more secure. Still, I can easily imagine that a man twenty years younger than I would shudder at me, like Joseph once did, if I were to forget myself & act like Potiphar['s wife] with him. Even my brownish skin must add to this effect, since it has begun to darken in the place where my neck rests upon my breast, and can no longer bear the pale powder that my "brightened" hair demands. But my eyes still shine darkly within their incense burners, and between them my blonde nose stands out, with all the allure of contrast. To do justice to my eyes it should really turn nobly upwards, but it juts straight out into the air instead. It is not because I have no illusions about friendship that I describe all this to you so objectively, but rather because I am convinced that it is not such a terrible thing; there are only two mistakes that one should not make: either not notice it, or become blind out of disgust. Then at least something good will come out of it. My husband must have seen every detail of my body by now, and he loves me anyway; he loves me as I am. Sometimes that makes him unbearable to me. For it takes all my power from me. I should say, it takes all the fantasizing out of my body. Then I am like a finished book, one that has already been declared to be very beautiful; for, the fact that a book is beautiful is no consolation for its having already been read.

And now I am reminded that I still owe you an answer to your question: It is naturally all the same to me *what* I read. I need the first fifty pages, perhaps, to get immersed in a book, and during that time I am still sensitive to the greater or lesser skill of the author. But after the first fifty pages I simply burn with excitement that I still have three hundred unknown pages before me, or even just three; it doesn't matter, just as long as I still see one page ahead. The book doesn't even have to be suspenseful; rain drops drumming on the window pane are less edifying but much more suggestive than Beethoven. Incidentally, I do not mean to present myself as a model reader here, but when I am on the last page I see every writer as a betrayer. Also in a man, the most important thing is that he allows us to be *possible* to the highest degree — as long as he is not fulfilled by us. Because I am convinced — though you must not tell anyone, for

I cannot prove it — that even Napoleon would have been very disappointed as a young man if someone had prophesied that he would someday be just the king of the French & not king of the world, pope, the first man to fly, etc. Yes, that his decline began in his first moment of self-satisfaction. What did we learn in our natural history lessons? Nature wastes millions of seeds, just so that a single goal can be reached.[1] Thus monogamy is really a debased form of fornication, against nature.

A person who observes with only one eye has a long look; it moves along like a fingertip over the face and the body. I sensed a powerful curiosity — not to touch me, that would have been an indiscretion, which the well-bred stranger would not have allowed himself — but to carefully explore me. One moment he was here, the next there; sometimes his indiscretion was unbelievably indiscrete; the prettiness of it was that one experienced the intellectual effort involved. I opened or closed my fur and my silk shawl, revealed parts, propped up my arm or let it fall in my lap. I imagine I challenged the stranger quite a bit in his attempt to make a picture of the whole from outlines and details. And I can only assume that he created me in the most skillful fashion, while we both had no preconceived idea of what the ultimate conclusion would be. Do you remember having read in Nietzsche: "Everything good makes me fruitful; that is the only form of gratefulness that I know"? That is a wonderful sentence — for women who want no children.

From time to time 'Manni' asked me if he should pass me another book or some sweets or a bottle of something: an abyss lay between us. On the other side of this abyss I found myself with the stranger. But see, we were coming closer to our destination, and my husband became agitated with preparations for our arrival. He opened all the little suitcases, shut them, put them away, took them out, put them aside, et cetera; the suburbs flew by. And here comes the reason why I am writing to you today at all. Suddenly I thought to myself, what will the eye of the stranger say to all these openings revealed to him by my husband in such a naïve and tactless manner? But as I looked up I realized that the eye was no longer looking at us, but flew rather back and forth in the most worried way amid all the luggage of its master. And then I noticed for the first time that I myself had been occupied for quite a while with nothing but my little golden pocket mirror, powder puff, & the rest of that "cat's toilette" that has become so unconscious with us. I had, in fact, totally forgotten the stranger.

And this is really quite a remarkable ending. No one was waiting for me and I was making myself up for no one, while the concrete, the real man across from me, who already had had his hand on the latch, could only think me silly for it. Or I had burned the dove in the pan on the stove, because sparrows were sitting on the roof. Not even for that reason, but just for one common sparrow, who in his commonality was only a fiction.

I really had to think this over. And as I did, an old but very fitting example came to me. After all, it is really quite similar to the men's game of the armaments industry, which carries on without any particular planned war, but just as a common custom; at most an incident occurs once in a while. Men are much more like us than we think.

SUSANNA'S SECOND LETTER[2] (OUR MEN)

My Dear! I find that our men have run astray into errant ideas, and it has provided me much diversion in recent years to ask how they can have arrived at them. They are fully incapable of managing their lives with these ideas & have a great fear of them, which they call admiration. In reality it is like this: if I catch my chambermaid letting herself be kissed by my male friend, my husband is furious and doesn't know if he should fire the girl right off or banish my friend from the house for "subversion of authority," "tactless negligence of sovereignty," and a dozen or so other reasons. He gets an overwrought head when he considers how many requisite proprieties are injured by such behavior. And when I finally say, "Do you know, Manni, the smartest thing is to act as if we knew nothing about it," a stone falls from his heart. But he looks at me angrily and says, "You women have no sense of responsibility for the commonality."

And, as far as it applies to me, he is right. I once had a friend who was a physicist, and he liked to listen to me describe what my friends were doing. He told me that each of the strangely tattooed symbols that he calls mathematics had helped him to write out a general short formula on the basis of which he could interpret, no matter when, and without trouble, any number of possible particular events, which otherwise, as single phenomena, he could never come to the end of. I can accept that. But what are general propositions worth that only offer a prohibition in every particular case? And all propositions that Manni calls "responsibility for the commonality" are of this sort.

My dear, this question is of great interest for us women. Manni says: "Thou shalt not kill." But only with great trouble did I manage to dissuade him from believing that a man may[3] kill the "thief of his honor" if he catches him red-handed. I really could not convince him. Luckily, "noble criminals of passion and honor" simply went out of fashion in the decade before the war, which aided my case. Just the same, Manni suffered terribly from philosophy during the war. Recently we had a nice young person at our table who had been caught up in a so-called scandalous affair not long before. That is to say, he rode off with a somewhat silly woman & her money, "invested" the money with the woman's approval, and then left her "high and dry" without her approval. For both instances there were sufficient reasons, but in the moment of dénouement the case was still unexplained and landed, alas, in the papers. "Really, one shouldn't associate with that sort of person," said Manni, after he had lunched with us. "But he didn't do anything to you," I replied. "In fact, you concluded a very profitable bit of business with him." "Yes," said Manni, "he did no harm to me; but even if he had harmed my enemy, I ought not to ignore it, insofar as I would condemn the same action directed at me!"

"But in this case the same action directed toward you is impossible in advance!"

"Always act," said Manni, "so that your personal action could be a general law..."[4]

"But there cannot be a law" — I said — "then for that to happen there would have to be a random meeting of this money, these conditions, this woman, & this man. And at least the last of these is a nice, idiosyncratic boy who doesn't run around in a sufficient number of examples to make up a law!" Then Manni "got his general head on" and dissected the case into a whole slew of general & irrefutable laws, each one larger than the other. But he could not make a case by putting them all together again. Men are always this way. They can easily prove that something is property or that it is theft, that someone is a spy or that he is a hero, that someone else is a power-monger or a brute: but when it comes to the either-either or-or, then they swindle just like women. They construct the world out of nothing but general rules and are forced to leave out the exceptions after the fact to make the case add up. Manni demands that the state do more for the Christian ethos, but he himself never goes to church and all his business friends are Jewish; he finds it good that we live in a modern &

democratic time, but under no circumstances will he forget that there are lords, princes, counts, eminences, etc. in it. He honors what is great in life, but he knows that the source of life simmers in the darkest corner, where it is powered by the bludgeons of egoism; he says that only generals believe in the possibility of war anymore, and he doesn't believe in the generals, but in all cases he lets them decide. My dear, it is a difficult world, a world of men, in which every statement is crossed out repeatedly, but none are completely erased. I am convinced that without exceptions this world would have stopped moving a long time ago, and would not have been capable of existing for a day. Really the world is roused by evil & uses virtue only as a restraint, without admitting it. Between you and me, I am also convinced that the great war of men only broke out because they did not know their way around their own peace anymore. They fled directly from this peace into that war. And if I consider what happened afterwards in the whole world — the way they contemned the shirkers and profiteers for so long, then turned around and called them clever and successful men — then it seems to me that we come to less harm through our immorality than our morality, which exists, between heaven & hell, nowhere on earth.

But if I say anything like this to Manni, he gets as angry as a boy whose school regulations have been contradicted, and declares that it is altogether impossible to play with girls. How much more clever are amorous women than men of character! "Every last fact is only the first of a new series. Every general law only a special part of an even more general law that will soon unfold. A man ends his story — how masterful! How conclusive! How it lends things a new appearance! Just look! There on the other side another one rises and draws a circle around the circle, which just now had been praised as the limit of creation!"[5] This remark is not mine, but it contains a consummate justification of so-called unfaithfulness. And we know quite well that it is not the same when two people do the same thing. A man can do us ill, yet through his manner while doing it, he charms us, & another, who can do us only good, will nevertheless fill us with disgust. The whole is always the decider, the ineffable balance. Never do we construct our justifications to ourselves from uniformities and generalized particulars. Sometimes I have a great desire to deliver a lecture about it to Manni, but I don't like speaking to him too openly about moral matters. You must therefore forgive me if I have misused this letter to you like this.

PAGE FROM A DIARY

One doesn't have to have lived long before remembering experiences that do not happen anymore.

In my childhood a strange occurrence was often repeated: a woman holds a fish firmly and it wiggles in her hand while she slices its belly open with her other hand. In my memory they are always large women whose faces & peaceful bosoms express goodwill and patience, and they wear white aprons. Such a thing no longer exists. If anything at all like this were to occur in the kitchen today, the women would be gaunt, with short hair, short skirts, and boyish movements; in a word, it would not be the same thing happening at all. At most, the woman's face might have the expression of a boy who is torturing an animal. I don't believe that such a picture could compress the heart so foolishly and incomprehensibly as what happened twenty years ago.

I know that this old memory would be explained today as a definitive expression of childhood sexuality, wherein the desire for the motherly woman is united with a suggestion of slimy repulsion and the crushing feeling of taboo, of authority, & of one's own smallness.

But if Schopenhauer had already known about psychoanalysis, he would have countered that this gruesome boyish feeling of lust — a mixture of insufficiency and desire — does not indicate a masochism that today is hardly traceable, but rather a sense of the true nature of love: "Overcome the secret" — he would have said — "and close the book of love, & you will notice that this picture was the only thing that was ever in it. The picture where you, free-willing un-free man, wriggle in the hand of the unwitting woman who holds you firmly & who eviscerates a piece of your great, terrible, happy vanity, which all of her forerunners have already feasted on." — He was a hater of love, this great writer, & only sounds like a woman-hater because he was a man.

But how — if this is the nature of love — does the woman adumbrate it? I asked M.[6] She didn't have anything to say against Schopenhauer. Only the roles were reversed; for a woman, when she comes into the years of woefulness and wisdom, also knows the feeling that she has wriggled in vain in the arms of men. But M. was very prejudiced against psychoanalysis. She maintained that it was a spruced-up invention of men. Few women have been active in it; the majority of them only in the passive role of patients. She can't bear this assembly of trimmers and dreamy men with their furious red heads. It would not be surprising, by the way, if the feminine fantasy turned out to be the fantasy of men about feminine fantasies. At the very least it is sifted, filtered, &

colored by a preponderance of works from the masculine imagination.

We came to speak of this as we were walking along the Danube Canal. It was in Vienna, during Christmas week. The hazy, festive, uncertain mist over the water's mirror was beautiful. Black-brown, high-sided ships, whose tops projected over the wharf. Great vessels by the shore, swarming women, men in wool vests with happy red hands fishing out of vats. Poor big fish, gasping for breath; weighed in hands; stuffed into cooking sieves. One could sense how much their grey silver bodies, the bow-shaped resistance of their muscles in the assessing hands, how much their torment belonged to the pleasure of the day. M. found nothing remarkable about the fact that women kill fish; somebody has to be the one to prepare these poor animals for the frying pan — assuming that one accepts eating them. She had friendly curious eyes, & all women, whether with short or long hair, with motherly or boyish bodies, looked in this moment exactly like she did.

I remember that I said that to her. A much simpler and more common cross-section of human interests lay exposed here than the one of which we had spoken earlier; more or less social prehistoric rock made up of baking, eating, & enjoying oneself; people embracing each other without affectation is part of this too. Above this and beyond this the complications, the meanings, the inhibitions & accelerations, urgings, difficulties, blissful feelings, vanities and deadly conflicts wander & change places, coming together and dispersing. From an unusually simple landscape mist arises, creates cloud castles of shifting form that slowly change. But for a long time they lend the landscape the character of the picture that they themselves crown. I don't know if that is very clear, but precisely these words occurred to me just then, and I believed, as I spoke them, that I was seeing the cloud castles of the centuries rising up out of what at bottom is always the same recurring human flatness.

M. didn't answer. But after a while she said, out of context: "I only had one single experience that could be compared to yours with the fish cooks, and it is very different. I was a small girl, when my father's father died and papa went away. I had not really understood why he had left all of a sudden, and only when he returned did he explain to me what had happened in detail. I didn't know very much about my grandfather, and the conversation in the family room in mother's presence made no real impression on me. But as my father tried to describe how grandfather looked when he found him on his death bed — at this moment my father threw his arms onto the dining room table, buried his face in his arms, and broke out into heavy sobs. I had never seen a man cry before and I thought that I was sinking. The quivering face of my dear crying father, his beard suddenly strange, tore my heart in two!"

"That also cannot be experienced today anymore," we both said at the same time, "because fathers no longer have beards!" We laughed or smiled about it. I don't remember anymore. But I remember exactly how it felt. A snowy wind was coming down from the mountains and thawing over the water, and warmth came off of our faces and froze in the silver cool mist. It made the world so uncertain. We felt our faces melting or petrifying in the air, without being able to distinguish between the two, and because of this our words gained more meaning than their content probably merited.

THE FAIRYTALE OF THE TAILOR

I.

I don't believe that he was a tailor. He stood before the judge and said:

"I want to be in jail; jail is where I feel best of all now.

My mother has died, I have fallen out with my friends; alas yes, & I treated my mother not at all as I should have.

What is life worth?! But not everyone can commit suicide. Have mercy on me!

Have mercy on me, Your Honor, and lock me up forever! I would be happy about it! In jail I could work as a tailor & would no longer need to go out into the world."

But the judge did not understand him, and was satisfied with a one-week imprisonment.

But the condemned man appealed the punishment on the grounds that it was insufficient.

Insufficient punishment can only be appealed by the State's Attorney, the judge told him.

But the State's Attorney did not care to appeal.

II.

I believe it was soon after this that I rolled a large bomb across the Ring of November 12th.[7] It was larger than myself. I had worked on it my whole life. I wanted to blow my epoch up into the air with it. A guard stopped me and looked at the bomb. I said: I must explode my epoch into the air with it, because they don't understand me. Officer, these are my works. At that moment the bomb even seemed to me to be as large as those giant rolls of paper that are piled up outside the newspaper printers. "Oh, you are from the newspaper..." said the officer tenderly, "You don't need a pass."

III.

My bomb rolled with a wonderful swerve through the archway under the Parliament ramp, into the great hall, where the many guards always sit when a revolution is threatened. I was allowed to light it, but it went out, because people were talking above me. When I cried out: "This will be a bomb twenty years after my death!" all the guards attacked me. I had an instrument — I think it is called a chest drill; it is a borer, which one holds against one's chest and works with a hand crank; one bores holes with it into iron. I defended myself with it.

I put it between the second & third button of a guard and cranked it. He became paler and paler. But the others tried to grab my arms, and though they were not immediately able to hold them fast, they became more and more entangled, which eventually kept me from continuing.

This is how I was arrested.

IV.

"Your Honor!" I said.

"Your Honor, I have studied a great deal and practiced, because I wanted to become a writer and to know my epoch, not only — ." I defended myself shamelessly, but the judge already knew that, smiled, & asked:

"Did you make money?"

"Never!" I exclaimed happily, "For that is forbidden!"

Then the first chairman looked the second chairman in the face, the lawyer looked at the lawless lawyer,[8] the State's Attorney looked at the court reporter, and all of them laughed. "I demand expert counsel!" called the defense attorney triumphantly.

"You are being charged because you make no money," said the judge.

V.

Since then I have been in prison.

He lacks money glands, is what the expert counsel said; because of this he lives without a moral compass and is immediately upset if someone treats him with disrespect; in addition, he suffers from thought flight. He cannot remember what others have told him a hundred times already; instead he is always looking for new ideas. And so on. The opinions of the literary experts were even worse. On the whole I am an inferior person who simply should not escape punishment.

But since it has come to this, I live in a fairy tale of orderliness. No one scolds me for unseemly behavior; on the contrary, among the other prisoners I stand out like a precious exception. My intelligence is superior. As a writer I am an authority, and am even allowed to write letters for the guards. Everyone praises me. I used to be an inferior person in the world of those who follow the rules of life correctly. Here, in the world of people who are incorrect, I am, according to the *consensus omnium*, a moral and intellectual genius. And I do nothing for money, only for praise & self-praise. I work as a tailor again. Magical essence of work, my soul is a needle; it flies in and out hour after hour, all day, it buzzes like a bee, and there is as little in my head as if I were laying in the grass and the bees were humming.

VI.

But if someone were to prove to me that none of this is true, and that I am not a tailor who was once inferior and that I do not live in a prison: then I would ask the President of the Republic for an honorary place in a madhouse.

It is nice there too. I would be fully up to the expectations, & no one would be surprised that I do what I do for its own sake. Yes, on the contrary, there they would even clear all obstacles out of my way.

ROBERT MUSIL TO AN UNKNOWN LITTLE GIRL

Unknown Little Girl!

Because I do not know you, I am writing to you through the newspaper. Indeed, as I reflect on the circumstances of our meeting, it becomes clear to me that I am writing to someone who no longer even exists or who does so only in the most shadowy sense. But our meeting took place under very ordinary circumstances. You walked into a streetcar where I was sitting. I presume that you would have noticed me among the few passengers, because you comported yourself for display with an uncommon poise, completely like a tiny little lady who senses that she is being observed. Accompanying you was a gentleman of my own age, who also pleased me well. He might have been a much older brother, but if he was your father, he acted toward you in a youthful and even-handed way and not at all masterfully. And I presume that you beguiled his fancy just as you did mine. I guess that you were at that time fourteen years old at most. You were wearing a velvet dress the color of the street. It fitted narrowly at the waist, so that the somewhat heavy but flexible material provided an illusion above & below of womanliness, without removing the childlike from the picture. The word "child-woman" came to me immediately when I saw you. Your velvet dress had fur cuffs on the tight sleeves and was trimmed on the bottom too, where it formed a broad hem in the shape of a wheel. It was somewhat reminiscent of a folk costume or an ice skating outfit; but it was probably not even a dress, but a coat. You yourself will certainly still know this today & happily remember it. I can only say in my defense that admiration observes much less precisely than self-admiration, which proceeds objectively in front of the mirror to examine and ascertain details.

Perhaps this excuse is faulty, but in any case, it acknowledges that my admiration was non-objective and romantic in a manner that is not entirely irreproachable, but also entirely natural. For the possibility of falling in love with you existed precisely in an action outside of a full consciousness of reality, which would not have allowed me to do so. Let us use that good old word dream for it: there one meets a person, recognizes who it is, and knows that it is someone else. In a similar way, deep within a mine above which we usually move, you remained for me a child but were also an extremely miniature woman — for ten minutes, before you exited the street car and were lost to me, without my doing anything to stop it. The way in which you entered, sat down, and handed the conductor the money somewhat lackadaisically (for it was you who did this, not your chaperone), was without any trace of the affectation with which a child does such things. And the features of your face, which I still see before me, with its dark ruddiness, its strong brows, and its slightly turned-up nose, were decidedly older than your years, but they nevertheless somehow formed something that was not merely the miniaturized face of a grown up woman. It occurs to me that your appearance can absolutely not be compared to a "bud," for the form of one of these is youthful to be sure, but hard & determined, and the amorous charm of your prematurely blooming childlike quality was more like a flower without roots, without stem.

I really have nothing more to say to you. And I have drawn neither a moral nor an anti-moral from it: obviously our meeting lay between these two possibilities, and since then more than ten years have passed without consequences. Sometimes you remind me that there are all sorts of stories of women who have originated mysteriously from tree branches, fountains, and alembics. Women who are not fully women and who stimulate men to invent fairy tales out of this not-fully. It is obviously a fantasy that goes to the heart of male persons for many reasons. And on the other hand, I ask myself what you still might know about this little girl, who will not have imagined becoming you, and who is, no doubt, somewhat disappointed by now.

Across Charlottenburg

Courtyards of the Kurfürstendamm

For now the only tree-level green hovering in the streets is the traffic lights, and there is something of last year, something almost ghostly in it, when it flickers life-like in front of three waiting cars, as if hundreds more were rushing behind them. The red leaves hanging on house after house telling us that apartments are for rent are very autumnal too. But in the courtyards of the crenelated palace apartments one recognizes spring by the lichened walls. The plaster has leafed off of the sides of the houses in large pieces; it had looked like a spreading rash, but now the sun shines on the sores. Only the chimneys, standing brotherly on the roofs, still have their color from the good old days, and when the sun shines on this whitish brick-red, one marks how solid the blue of the sky has become in the last few weeks. If one lowers one's eyes from this play of expansiveness down the walls, even the leafed-off flecks on the walls are capable of providing the illusion of a blooming unfolding life.

Around the Zoo

The color of early spring is brown, in countless shadings, from the colorblind sallow grass to the lustrous brown of the water. Only the naked branches of the weeping willow poke sharp, whip-thin green lashes into nature. A red patch — it is nothing but the red-painted head of a wooden post — seems like a blooming branch behind a shivering bush; a tilled flower bed: the heart is terrified by it, & reveals that it is filled with a readiness similar to that of the little ship in the sluice waiting for its "steam": the comfortable little coffee machine has had its old hulk and its chimney freshly painted with red and white stripes. For with every new spring it sets off on a great journey that lasts almost a whole year, although, year in, year out, it only rides back & forth between Charlottenburg and Stralau.

Charlottenburg Palace

The young conductor thinks he has discovered that we are foreigners because we ask him where we should disembark. So he gives us the friendly advice: "Do not miss a visit to the mausoleum: The 'reflex'[9] there is wonderful, it is the most amazing 'reflex' in all of Berlin!" I think that the essence of all fame and all tourist attractions must be closely related to this bit of advice.

Just the same, we don't want to see the mausoleum again, but rather the park, & in front of the park there hangs a sign that says, "closed today due to impassable paths." There had been no bad weather all week, and all of a sudden one feels as if one has been transported to the century of attentive authorities, who protect their citizens from dangers that lay hidden somewhere, although as far as the eye can see the paths seem to be in perfect order. In such cases, a contemporary person attempts to find some alternative route. This leads first of all past the Kaiser Friedrich monument, where people sit one beside the other with out-stretched legs and faces offered up to the heavens: entirely as if the sweep of a hand had strewn long-stemmed cut flowers all along the benches. Further on we can see from Tegel Way that the interior of the palace park is as dry as it is smooth, but our attention is immediately drawn to the opposite side, where, in an architectural style that is eclectic-Romanesque, but bulky just the same, a state courthouse threatens with the motto, chiseled in stone over the entrance, *Suum cuique*. That is, To each his own. And it is a good old Prussian, and also a very just, motto. But in the spring sunshine it suggests the reflection on whether some people might happily trade in their own — if it happens to consist of a number of years in prison — for a lighter sentence.

Siemen's City

After having weighed the difference between righteousness and self-righteousness, we find ourselves in a leafy field that, expressed politely, smells of the cycles of nature. But it shimmers just the same in all colors ranging from pink to dark blue. On the left, nearby, behind common factory courtyards, the Spree flows; on the right, the suddenly vast sky rests upon the tousled treetops of the meadow; but directly in front something super-human is growing — at least super-European — higher than a house, wider than a tower, constructed above the train tracks and ducts: one of the factory buildings of Siemen's City. The closer one comes, the stronger the impression. When one is finally standing right in front of it, there is nothing to these pinkish flanks but their purposefully rising life: defiantly, maybe even somewhat pretentiously (in their imperious upward expansion; but without a little pretentiousness one can hardly begin to think of monumentality), this beautiful gigantic child of technology and of joint-stock capital offers its well-proportioned athletic body to the heavens.

Hidden behind it: the real little Siemen's City: a rather humble affair by itself, a German town circa the year '90, with Lohengrin architecture and modern accoutrements.

The Little Colony

In the place where one has to wait for the connection, one is still standing under the earth; then, when the train comes out into the light and only the tops of the freely standing pines part in the sky, one feels just as if one were in Switzerland or in the Tirol, and as if one had just arrived at the height of the pass and the strong wind was blowing through the open window. We can assume that the true colonists experience this moment every day when they return "from the city." The overcast day, the ice-grey blanket of clouds, the little frozen lake, the streets that are still damp, the view of the receding factory smokestacks, the sand stirred up by the construction: nothing stands in the way, even here, of imagining spring. The chains of the city are broken; the human being stands amid something vaporously infinite. One feels it even if one has come out "just because"; and there must really be something special behind this miraculous illusion, something that drives the city to pursue the woods like a child chasing a bird, a bird which it wants to touch but always chases further away.

THE INN ON THE OUTSKIRTS[10]

At twelve midnight, no matter what night, the heavy wooden gate of the entrance was shut, and two arm-thick iron rods were lodged in place from the inside. From then on, a sleepy, rustic-looking maid waited for late arriving guests. After a quarter of an hour, a guard who had overseen closing time at the pubs passed by, making his slow, wide tour. Around one in the morning, from out of the mist, the crescendo of the patrol's tread, coming from the nearby holding barracks, echoed past and died down again. Then for a long time there was nothing but the cold damp silence of these November nights. Finally at three in the morning the first wagons from the country arrived. They dashed over the cobblestones, making a heavy racket; wrapped in their blankets, numb from the rattling and the morning cold, the drivers' corpses swayed behind their horses.

On a night like this, shortly before the midnight hour, the couple arrived and asked for a room. The maid seemed to recognize the gentleman. First, without rushing at all, she locked the high gate, laid the heavy crossbars in place, and led the way, without asking any more questions. A stone staircase came first, then a long windowless hallway, quickly and unexpectedly, two corners, then a stairwell with five stone steps worn-down by many feet, and again a hallway, whose loose tiles teetered under their soles. At its end, without the guests being at all astonished by it, a ladder of a few steps led up to a small floor area, opening onto three doors standing low and brown around the hole in the floor.

"Are these here taken?" asked the gentleman, pointing at the doors. The old woman shook her head no. Giving herself light with the candle, she unlocked one of the rooms; then she stood there with the light held high and let the guests enter. It did not often happen that she heard silk undergarments rustle & the scuttling of high heels that shrank in terror from every shadow on the tiles. "Oh, how eerie! eek, how romantic!" the lady exclaimed more than once, and the old woman, suspicious of the silken one, must have taken this to be a criticism. Fractious and obtuse, she looked the lady, who now had to walk past her, right in the face. In her embarrassment, the lady nodded at her condescendingly and must have been at least forty years old or a little older. "Everyone was young once," — thought the maid, — "or perhaps still with one's own husband, in God's name, if it comes to that; but a woman like this going off on an adventure!" Then she took the money for the room, extinguished the last light in the hallway, and retired to her chamber.

Shortly afterwards there was not a sound in the whole house. The light of the candle had not yet found the time to creep into all of the recesses of the miserable room. The strange gentleman stood like a flat shadow at the window, and the lady, in anticipation of the unknown, had sat herself down on the edge of the bed. She had to wait a torturously long time; the stranger did not move from his position. If things had moved quickly up to that point, advancing onward like a dream, now every movement stuck in a brittle resistance, which did not allow a single limb to loosen. He felt, this woman expects something from him. How dare she?! She expected to see him "at her feet." He knew, you should now "cover her with kisses." He became nauseous. Her dress was high-buttoned at the top, her hair artificial: to unbutton the dress was to unlock the unimaginable vault of a life's innards, the door of a prison. In the middle there stood a table; on top, the objects of her life, in slippers, making faces. He looked at it with hostility & fear. She wanted to catch him; her hand pushed his unceasingly towards the latch. In the end all that would be left would be to spring in like a grenade and to tear the wallpaper down in shreds! With the greatest strain he was finally able to wrest at least one sentence over these obstacles: "Did you notice me right away then, when I looked at you?" Ah, it worked. A fountain of speech overflowed. "Your eyes were like two blackthorn apples!" — Or had she said "stars"? — "Your wild mouth — ."

"And you were immediately gripped by passion?"

"But beloved! Would I be here otherwise?!" — Stress was laid on her counter question. What if she had fallen victim to a ruthless adventurer? She didn't know the man; clothing, gait, and face were elegant, and love is a passion! That was everything.

"I followed you; for days...!" said the stranger softly.

At this moment he felt that it was utterly impossible to take a bird in the hand. This naked skin was supposed to press itself on his naked and unprotected skin? His breast was to fill itself from hers with warmth? He tried to delay it with witticisms. They were tortured and nervous. He said: "Isn't it true, big women bind up their feet too? With their shoes. And there where the lace is, the flesh protrudes over a bit, and a faint unique aroma accumulates there. A small, wax-yellow aroma that exists nowhere else in the world? Undress!"

The unhappy woman, who, transported by a miracle, had kept her name secret, was outraged. "You are mistaken," she cried, "do not speak to me so familiarly, let me go; I am a respectable woman, a lady!"

"Forgive me!" said the stranger. He looked elegant and miserable again. Only a person capable of deep feeling could look like that. A person tortured by a great sinful passion. Leopold won't be home for two days; he can't understand me either — she thought — I should have called home in any case, to say I would be spending the night away. The blood that had risen to her throat in resistance plunged headlong back to her hips. The stranger held his hand over his eyes. She felt that she had been unfair to him. She rejoiced: jealousy? Sweet! Bitter! Must it not be difficult for him, without knowing her, to orient himself! She wanted to tell him that Leopold was really a good person — .

But the one who did not understand answered: "I envy you him." And with that statement motion entered his expression for the first time. His eyes burned like torches, and it seemed to her that he wanted to annihilate her with his words, so strangely did his look begin to smolder. He continued: "I was never jealous. I love rooms like this. Such a wretched chair. These sheets; perhaps an hour ago a fellow with smallpox lay in them!"

She smiled: "You are joking, wild one! You mischief! You just want me to feel the magnitude of the offering I am bringing to your beauty."

"No," said the man, "if you look at these two wax stumps, aren't they like two burnt-down limbs? They have been waiting here for you. Perhaps there are insects waiting for you in bed, they will hook themselves into the soft sweet dough of your skin and partake of you, while you forget yourself. I thank you that you have come. I only dare go out with such flaky, toothless, warty things. Tumbling senselessly — I assure you, sometimes quite senselessly tumbling. And if you do it quickly there will be a crack in me, yes, a crack, a terrible, wholly inhuman sound like a wagon wheel."

"He is a poet," she answered herself, "or a philosopher, they are like this nowadays; one must just leave it for now, later I will exert the power of the distinguished woman over him." She started to undress deliberately; she owed it to her honor.

Now he was frightened. The thought tormented him: wind up! Like a child's toy, until the gears, until all the gears engage.

And the second torment was: She is pursuing me. She is rolling herself out. Always right in front of me. What does she keep saying?! I am to throw myself like a dog upon the round, rolling ball of her life.

Now she sat in just shoes and stockings before him. She undressed entirely, because he had spoken of the insects. That seemed safer to her. Her hips rolled in bulging folds. She began to tremble.

His eyes pulled back & forth like a dog on its chain. "Won't you undress?" she asked.

"Don't you want to dance first?" asked the stranger.

Tears of fury came from somewhere. The lady regretted the adventure and would have sped away had she been able. But what was left to her now but to find him interesting and unconventional? *Ach*, love is really a lathering pony springing away, even when it shudders and stands still.

"You must dance wonderfully," he said, stalling again. "Sometimes music sits just on the precipice of being and blows over. But movement — !"

"No, I don't dance," she answered. "Be good, stop babbling such nonsense. I love you anyway, you naughty boy. Why don't you kiss me?!"

A silence followed. Then, carefully, he asked: "Have the little girls gone out, the ones who lived in your body?" But at the same time he heard himself say the meaningless sentence: "whoever loves is young," and in that moment her arms hung around his neck. His eyes darted back and forth like fish in the dark.

"Let your eyes be, beloved, beloved, you look so elegant & miserable!"

Then he lifted the burden up with the power of despair and kissed it. "How is your Confucius?" he asked softly. She took this to be a technical term from the world of men; she didn't want to lose her advantage; he was cozying up to her. A prophecy also told her: it will be better when we are further along. The tip of the man's tongue touched her lips. This ancient means of human communication, where foreheads always sit above such lips, was familiar to her. She spread out her tongue slowly and pushed it forward. Then she pulled it quickly back and smiled roguishly. Her roguish smile was — she was well aware — already famous when she was but a child. And she said, on the off chance, perhaps inspired by a subconscious connection of sounds: "Confucius is enjoying itself" —. Not even the softest thought betrayed that she had ever heard this word in any other context.

Then the unknown man sighed. The round ball of the world rolled over him. "Once more," he begged, with shaky knees. And then it took a long time until his teeth came all the way through her tongue. But finally he felt it thick in his mouth. The storm of a great deed eddied up within him. In its circling it swept the white bloody mass of the wretched woman away, flailing about herself in a corner of the room, screeching in the high hoarseness of a tumbling torso of sound.

BROKEN OFF MOMENT

It happened on the last day of the trial around three in the afternoon, shortly before the break that is supposed to take place after the interrogation of the witnesses, in order to give the judge, the prosecutor, and the defendant an opportunity to eat something before justice opens its mouth to pass judgment. The June day hauled itself across the morning, piled up with heat like a hay wagon that slowly comes closer; though one thought one heard its rumbling, only the shadow of its warmth fell in the small courtroom, whose windows looked gloomily upon the glaring rows of houses across the way. The people who had business in the room would have preferred an all-out heat to this insidious one, and there was no one who did not think from time to time about the countryside & vacation.

A few dozen landscapes were hidden in their heads. A river bank with a small bathing cabana; a gulp of milk, whose genuine taste had once made a suspicious impression, but now streamed down one's throat like the peacefulness of paradise; a mountain train station, before which the hotel porter stands in the morning coolness with hobnailed boots and a golden-braided cap; stupid or meaningless details, whose origin no one can tell. But they always come when one has enough of so-called higher efforts, and the conclusion of the legal battle was one of these. The plaintiff, who was not very likable, fought for honor and position — he was being accused of some dirty business, and he probably had done it all too, but he still felt himself to be the victim of his exposer. For weeks he had contrived for himself the role of an persecuted innocent man, & the thought that he would either kill himself or his enemy if the trial turned out badly had impelled him, at the beginning of the proceedings, to carry a pistol with him. Since then he had never been separated from it & had vaguely felt that it kept him from behaving correctly, though he hadn't ever really wanted to use it in earnest, and the thought of killing himself had only occurred to him because he had not been able to imagine what else he would do. For he is neither brave, nor does he feel young enough to begin again, but without the pistol he would have become more determined to defend the place which he still had held at the beginning of the trial, before he had committed a series of mistakes and revealed a number of weaknesses during the hearing. And for hours now it had been certain that the end must be shameful, and as the judge called the last witness of the day, a man from whom he could only expect something bad, he had whispered "Now!" and grabbed his pocket with the same feeling as if he were supposed to deliver a speech & could not remember a word of it.

But he let it go again, and as time marches forward, he tries to rouse himself once more by thinking of his wife and children, who would innocently suffer if they declassified him. He plays nervously with his hands, but really his hands play with him, for there is still something hidden in them that they have not yet done. In the meantime, in his agitation, instead of the peace of death, he longs unconsciously for the peace of the first day of vacation, when one climbs out of that part of today that is still today, as one climbs out of clothes one has worn too long.

His opponent, in contrast, knows much better what it is he is after: he wants to cleanse the occupation to which they both belong of a "vermin." And he proceeds with a plan and with force, by providing evidence of the truth of the scandalous allegations that had forced him to mount the prosecution. He is unswerving. But even he does not have the fresh hate of the morning of the first day. And once in a while an astonishment creeps over him that he has gotten himself so mixed up in something that is otherwise foreign to him. But his carefully collected store of evidence is inexhaustible and overflows by itself from behind every pardon, and the unfamiliar noble condition of finding himself defending his occupation from someone "ignoble" lends him a certain Sunday feeling, if perhaps only a Sunday evening feeling, when one already thinks quite happily about the freshly commencing week days. Also, the mood in the courtroom, which is filled for the most part with people who are connected professionally to the two opponents, is similar. It is almost anxious. With every vileness that is denounced, dignity is spindled to an even more suspended state as they feel themselves insulted; the people sit quietly and outraged; they feel justified in their indignation, but as it becomes greater with every half hour, they start to feel as volatile as one does when one no longer sees the ground below one. The "ignoble one" feels this; even the judge's view can hardly be altered now. He sees his opponent standing in front of the window like a solidly intact body & hates him up to his mouth, but he hardly resists at all anymore. In this moment there is no one in the room who would not think that the next and last half hour will conclude the trial. The proceedings are somewhat reminiscent of a steamboat's last maneuver as it comes into dock, which can only be followed by throwing and fastening the rope and pulling it onto land. Even the ostracized one is convinced & feels that it is now too late for everything that he might have done.

And precisely there the moment springs out of order, six moments — six shots break off. A swirling fragment of time. No one knows anymore how it broke itself off, after it is over. The uncertain one, the fired pistol in his hand, finds himself silent, positioned as if he feared a beating from the one who has collapsed beneath his shots. But suddenly he turns with the raised weapon toward the judge's bench and cries out two times:

"Your Honor, Your Honor, it is too late, it is too late!" The judge stares at the pistol and growls: "Put that down!" Finally the guards manage to separate their soles from the floor to fall upon the murderer. As they reach him and grab him by the shoulders he collapses & they have to let him sit on a bench for a while, where he silently stares straight ahead before they can lead him away. The dead man lies face down on the ground in a small puddle of blood. The audience has sprung over the benches and surrounded him; one of them repeatedly tries to lift the corpse's head, blood drips over his fingers; but when the murderer is led past the corpse and away, the man lets the head drop, jumps up, and stumbles two steps after him, screaming: "Murderer!" A second remains kneeling, but raises his hands with spread fingers and also screams "Murderer!" And others too come out of the unfamiliar state they were in for a few moments after the shots ripped through the room, and begin to scream.

But the murderer suddenly begins to tremble at this apparently highly futile statement, and tears begin to fall from his eyes, which bit of naturalness brings everyone back to a more normal condition, so that they quickly become sober.

THE STORM TIDE ON SYLT

On the 30th of August, the well-known resort island Sylt was surprised by a storm tide of such great force that nothing of its kind had been remembered for decades; and it arrived therefore quite unexpectedly.

Unusual weather came first. Aside from short gusts of wind, storms are supposedly not known on this island, because due to certain atmospheric conditions, they are usually concentrated on its southern tip, and usually sweep across both sides of the island over the Northern and the Wadden Seas, & then move on. But this time a steadfast southwest wind raged through the island for many nights of heavy storms; late mornings — rain without ceasing, clearing afternoons, eerily clear evenings and mornings. Some guests had left unusually early this year because of the weather, others because of the rise in transportation prices in Germany. In the last few days the island seemed to have been returned to itself & to its lonely, fantastical peculiarity. In the night preceding the storm tide, lightning struck the island & burned a farmhouse down. And, cut off from the life of the bathing season and the holiday and dollar-enthusiasm of the departed city people, this insignificant occurrence took on all the weight that it can have for lonely inhabitants who repeat to each other with horror that such an accident had not occurred for twenty-seven years. It hit a small Frisian house from the 18th century that had been renovated into a summer residence, which stood, as they do here, brick-red with white window frames on green lawns, hidden behind walls of mud and stone, with old glazed tiles and old furniture, the high thatched brow of its roof deeply receding. I understood why the people didn't go to bed on this night of storms, and why lights glimmered hauntingly behind the windows of all the houses, none of which — with the exception of those in the southern parts — had protection against lightning. We stood about, hands in our pockets, and peered into this fire that even the strong rain could not extinguish, we few summer guests from the neighboring houses, with the firemen, who poked with their staves here and there in the glowing rafters or sprayed a little water as if out of a garden hose. Beneath the gigantic cloud-filled sky everything looked almost sweet and miniature. The only thing that made an uncanny impression was the way the fire hissed from beneath the house door under pressure from the wind as if it were coming from out of a smithy's hearth.

The wind swelled as the night wore on and the next day it was unfurling thickly across the island. Storms up in the mountains crash and churn, but this one was like a vast, almost placid stream, trembling from internal shocks alone. Up on the dunes one could hardly keep one's eyes open, and on the heath behind the dunes the people tumbled in their colorful wool jackets hither and thither like a vibrating field of flowers. At three in the afternoon the storm tide came. We fought our way to the shore and watched as the water rose ever higher hour by hour. First it devoured the sand castles & the wide bathing beach, then it took the beach baskets, which we thought we had brought to safety on the partial elevation of the vertically inclining island wall; taken by the waves, one after the other, they flopped into the water like gigantic seals. This all was just a game, but it gave some preliminary notion of the elementary forces at work and perpetrated considerable damages. But at three o'clock, when the storm tide should have begun to recede, it did not; instead it strengthened, agitated further and further by the powerful wind. The "sea cliff" that rose along the shore for a lengthy extension, a wall with a Homeric silhouette, ten to thirty meters high, made of layers of sand, earth, and clay, rising from out of the sand of the island, was dashed up to half its height with masses of water; and gigantic masses of earth, torn apart by rain, besieged by the waves as if by battering rams, were broken off from Sylt in pieces many kilometers long.

The catastrophe did not, however, occur here, or on the coast that was exposed to the pressure of the storm tide, but, surprisingly enough, on Wadden. In the southern direction behind Westerland, Sylt is shaped like a pair of large opened pincers; between its two arms lies the Wadden Sea, practically enclosed by the High Sea. At low tide it retreats far from the shore and resembles a large swamp. It seems that this relatively small mass of water, which received the massive force of the North Sea's shocks, responded with an especially vehement vibration. The island flattens out completely here from a height of a few meters and ends in the so-called marshes, an area that serves as grazing land and that lies almost directly at sea level. The storm tide forced its way, apparently following the hollow of some streams, into this piece of land with a terrific violence, and covered it for many kilometers with the surge of the sea. This breach continued for many hours; the farmsteads mounted a resistance and finally an embankment held it back, but it was so unexpected that along with vast stretches of crops, much livestock fell victim to it, and a few people were drowned.

The next day, as these excesses of bad weather subsided, everything looked merely a little rained upon. Some puddles were left; the remains of the harvest cleaved to the ground; farmers gathered their wheat and hay; the enclosures of Westerland were hardly damaged. In other places, clods of earth lay on the beach; a few enthusiasts had already built new sand castles. In the south, two kilometers from the shore, I found a little drowned field mouse cast up by the waves, with drenched fur:

this was all that the storm tide had left behind on the site of the catastrophe for the curious observer; its more precious victims had already been dragged away by the current of the sea's receding tide.

THE THIRSTY ONES

He was called Ali and had willingly attached himself to us some time before the murder; we didn't know where he came from, and we believed that he belonged to one or another of the farms that lay scattered across the branching slopes of the mountains. The name Ali was a free invention, a poetic creation, one could say. The teacher made it up suddenly when their eyes dove into each other's for the first time. And because this name was somewhat unfitting and irrational, but had made its authority felt so forcefully from within, we all had the feeling that a poem had occurred to the teacher, and we were amazed. We all insisted on calling him Ali, and he didn't object, as if it had always been his name. And in the afternoon we five came out of the tavern, down the bumpy stone path to the torrent — or whatever one called this deserted triangle where the mountain stream, leaving its own wild valley, shimmies out and stirs into the great fecund central valley, before it is taken up again by the small, quick, civilized river which even in its beginnings had a name famous throughout Europe.

"I can't stand this primitive triangular condition any longer!" I ranted. "Everywhere that Nature appears in simple geometric forms it is treacherous; lakes round like circles are fathomless, volcanos are cone shaped..." — I searched for more evidence, but could think of none. — "Gall stones are cubes with sanded off corners" — added the silk spinner. — "Avalanches are tablets," added the railway man, who had learned to ski while studying law for three semesters. "And you are all knuckle-headed squares," said the teacher, ending the discussion, "you forget that the whole earth is round!" He was the strong man.

However the case may have been in truth, every time we skirted the torrent, a desolate impression mingled with our own moods. We avoided the path — gravelly as if it too were a dried up stream — that cut across the triangle; we sprang clumsily over the stony ditches where the stream had evaporated during the dry season; held each other by the wrists so that we would not be dashed back against the bushes in case of a full-on attack, and we all tumbled on; howling, as if there were no people for miles around within this ten-minute swath of desert, and with our lurching we scared away the sheep that grazed on the small islands of grass. Ali was especially dangerous in this. He thrilled with pleasure; we whistled & screamed "Ali!" and jumped a meter high so we wouldn't lose sight of him, and out of fear that he could really catch a sheep and tear it apart. And we thrilled too.

Because, in contrast to us others, Ali was a dog, a Venetian hound, or so the teacher, whom we could not contradict in questions of natural history, assured us, and besides, Ali had run after him and not us. He was not very tall, but had a broad & robust build, with the big friendly ears of a hunting hound, crooked strong legs, and short fur with big white and brown patches that would have made it like a chestnut if the white parts had not also been sprinkled with black like a speckled horse. And if Ali had killed one of the sheep, we would have been put in a very bad situation, since the little city began less than a hundred feet behind the torrent. It was no bigger than a market town, but was so tidy and inhabited by such wealthy citizens that it had the status of a city. We always shook our trousers straight behind the last bushes, brushed the dust off our shoes a bit, let the wildness disappear as quickly as possible from our faces, & called Ali to follow close on our heels for the length of the respectable shop-lined street, before we reached the other side of the country road that led to the sea & new pleasures.

If one were to take a map of Europe and point to the place where this city lay with the tip of the finest needle, even this small point would cover much more than this city and the substantial mountains that meant sunrise and sunset to its inhabitants. There was little hope that we would ever come out of here as young men. Once a week the illustrated newspapers arrived, with pictures from all over the world. Skyscrapers and speeds of 200 kilometers, naked dancers and elegant ladies' underwear, great charlatans and safaris to Africa, suicides under the spell of cocaine, & high society marriages. We knew all the technological jargon of the elegant life, & our eyes soaked the pictures in, as if we had swallowed glittering gems that did not budge in our bodies, neither forward nor backward, ever after. I believe nothing could have held us back from becoming a robber band and capturing the world, except that we didn't know how to begin. Those of the group who were born here felt very differently about it than we did; once in a while they drove to the nearest big city — whence the merchants travel to the next-nearest larger one — and one of them brought back a fashionable necktie with a sheepish grin, another one brought back a much worse keepsake, and a third even brought back a little automobile. Thus the clever little city gradually brought modern times upon itself, and in the end one lived not entirely without little adventures and secret scandals between its walls. But we scoffed; we declared that the automobile was a passé, out-moded type; we were driven by fury.

Back then, on the day when the little accident — the murder — happened, we had just come out of the torrent again and were directly facing the first of the isolated little houses where the poor people and railway workers lived, when Ali ran ahead of us and was already sniffing the walls & the doorsteps. Ali, who had been driven from his home by a love of adventure, although we only had shouting and blind commotion to offer him. Unsuspecting, we watched and listened to him at his business, barking at a tiny little dog who darted out of a house and played the cantankerous home-owner, puffing himself up & yielding no space at all to the stranger, despite the fact that underneath all this fuss he gave the impression of being quite friendly; an utterly inelegant little mutt, with dirty pale-blond hair, who would probably have liked to play if one only allowed him to satisfy his duty as man and father of the house first. But Ali had had enough. The little one's pale-blond tail — the silk spinner reported this later — had just moved to the side to wag. But before he was able to complete even the first half of this swing that would make his canine smile spread over his entire backside while his front portion still snarled, Ali bit the little one, disregarding all manners, in the nape of his neck, shook him back and forth twice between his chops and spit him out onto the ground. A miserable, short lament tore through our ears, followed, before we could run toward them, by an eerie silence. And there the dog lay in front of the house, with the stiff, somewhat ridiculous and somewhat moving look of a corpse, while Ali moved away from our circle.

It was remarkable that this little event, which a cheerful & content person would hardly have wasted a shoulder shrug of pity on, gripped us as unexpectedly as if it had been a stroke of lightning. We were transformed.

"You have to hit him!" I yelled to the teacher in incomprehensible agitation; all the others screamed too, as if from out of one mouth: "You have to hit him!" The teacher seemed to be overcome by the same conviction; as if in a heavy dream, he took a loop of vine and called Ali over. Hardly a single sound of pain escaped him during the punishment; in order to receive it he had laid himself down on the ground and suffered it like a warrior of noble breed. But as the delivered pains continued too long in answer to our cries of encouragement and, obviously, in his opinion, overstepped the boundaries of a just atonement, he began at first to growl and then to bare his teeth. "You have to keep hitting him!" we cried, and the teacher, who seemed to be ready to stop, actually kept going. But the more threatening Ali looked, the slower the blows fell. They seemed as pedagogical as if they wanted to hit their mark precisely, but in truth they were hesitant. He was a strong young man, the teacher, with a thick head of hair; I had always taken him to be a rough fellow, but now I noticed from behind, without looking him in the face, that he was afraid and made of soft flesh.

With that the unexpected event was really over. Because a haggard, ill-humored looking woman came from behind a corner of the house with an earthenware crock on her arm. We feared that she was the owner of the dirty little dog and that she would raise a great hue and cry that could lead to incalculable consequences, for we were not particularly beloved in the little city; and suddenly we took to our heels. First with dignified slowness; but no sooner were we hidden by one house than we began to trot; and as we came into view again a little way off, we fell into a gallop, now altogether brazenly, in diagonal leaps that were supposed to look like innocence, but which really were concerned with putting space between us and the misdeed as quickly as possible. But there was no sound audible behind us. And as Ali, who at first had trotted behind us morosely, saw us running and jumping, he shook off his bad mood, sprang ahead of us, nudging each of us with his snout, making the dust fly, our leader in the direction of the city.

The cornfields, higher than a man, lay on the other side. If one sweeps through them with a guilty conscience, they whisper in the most astounding way. And then came the sea; then the path up the mountainside. Through the forest of chestnut trees. And oaks. The sea sinks down ever deeper. But none of us ever got beyond the inn along the way, where there were loaves of bread and wine. The heat of the day glowed upon our faces, and the heat of the wine rose in them slowly like the moon among the clouds. Below the trees it grew dark; a storm lantern was placed upon the stone table. People said that the path led further on to wild cliffs, then over the mountain into the great valley. Agnese said this, the innkeeper's daughter, whose lover we didn't know, but presumed to be a stately man who would have no time for us. And with moon and wine, and the tension of the day melting away, the unadorned thought — that we had hidden from each other until then — the thought of Ali's murder, came out.

"It wasn't 'fair' of him, with such a difference in size!" — one of the railway men, who set store by sportsmanship, suggested, to excuse our horror. "An unfair fight is revolting!" — but his explanation garnered no approval. Someone else said: "If it had only been a cat!"; but no one was capable of relieving us of the unforgettably revolting sensation left behind by this event. A silence ensued. Finally someone said slowly: "But it didn't revolt us at all. We enjoyed it." That was it. We trod upon our hearts and slipped on them, as the cry of the unspeakable rang in the air, and now we wanted to kick them away, as if we had accidentally slipped on an orange peel.

"If he were a person, it would only be a matter of manslaughter in the heat of passion!" — added the silk spinner. "Three years in prison; that's it!" The teacher challenged the evasion. "You can't judge an animal as you would a person." He was suddenly worried that we could gang up on Ali in this mood.

A pause, and then all of a sudden one of us asked crudely: "Do you know that so precisely?!" — There we were again, where we needed to be.

"He doesn't know anything!" yelled the silk spinner, suddenly leaving the teacher in the lurch. "Any of us could bite someone in the nape of the neck ourselves

& shake him dead between our teeth!" — He gave no further explanation, and fell silent. Everyone looked at him with astonishment. The rich silk spinner was the only one of us who came from a family in this little city and he looked as if he could bite through the neck of a chicken. Unfortunately, we were unable to contradict him, but the difference between our agreement and distinct disgust was very slight.

"Then why did all of you insist that I hit him?" the teacher now asked, ruefully.

Yes, why? One of us pushed his chair back and said, while standing up: "How much longer do we have to stay in this damned hole of a city!?"

I took the storm lantern & shined it under the table where Ali was sleeping. We looked at him. He woke up and stretched his good-humored paws, the big skin flaps of his jowls hung innocently over his teeth. "Ali!" we cajoled. Agnese stood there in the doorway, her arms crossed, & watched us. She always stood like that and watched us, as our words sometimes stalled, sometimes climbed up to the stars like mist over a waterfall. We didn't even know if she understood what we said; she never joined in; she just watched us, the way one watches animals or a silent movement; she seemed to despise us. I put the light back, & threw money on the table — that brought her to life. Ali had finished stretching & trotted in front of us on our way back to the city. He seemed to be satisfied with his day, & I believe that we others secretly envied him.

SMALL JOURNEY THROUGH LIFE

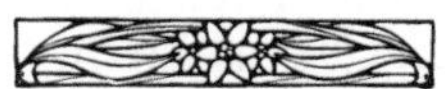 Life is full of miracles. They just happen to be paid for and already belong to someone else. But in Simmering there stood a Styrian wagon on the street, with a pony in front, and also a small wagon with an even smaller pony. Even I, whenever I see a pony, believe it belongs to me: the eyes look out so fiendishly-friendly behind its shaggy bangs; the whole creature is so small that one could slip it into one's hand; & the tail is so splendid. Why would the sultan have seven horsetails if there were not something in it?! And here I am, a thoroughly grown-up man. But the boys who suddenly saw the Styrian wagon with its little horse in Simmering were only nine or ten years old and were, moreover, just on their way home from school. This is how the miracle started; to wit, there was no one anywhere near the wagon to whom it could have belonged.

The boys climbed up, lifted the reins, and the pony began to move, in earnest — even to run, when they cracked the whip — and everything came true just as splendidly as in a fairy tale. Dogs had to get out of the way, people had to spring to the sides, even the guard at the street crossing had to give them a signal as he would to a real wagon owner. They headed for the Laaerberg section, then to the East Railway, across the racetrack into the elegant city, and when they finally arrived back on the grass behind the Simmering wagon factory, they unhitched the horse and let it graze. How! Even if we knew nothing more about them than that they let the horse graze, we would already know that these little thieving fellows were fairy tale boys from out of an Indian's wig-wam.

Did they get bored of it? They rode on, and, in the street called Brehmgasse, the inevitable fight broke out. One of them wanted to drive to the left, the other to the right. Then one of them wanted to sell the horse, and the other wanted to take it home. With that the miracle was over. Naturally all evil enters the world because of left and right. For, either everyone wants the same thing, and not everyone can have it, or one person wants to go left and the other wants to go right, and then only one of them is the stronger one. And soon a policeman arrived who, as is his duty, saw through everything, and today the miracle, along with the pony, is back with the person who paid for it, and the two boys have been dispatched to their parents and to the oversight of the juvenile welfare service.

It wasn't easy; what could they say to them? These two boys had driven from one end of life to the other. Should they tell them: fortune favors the brave? The world belongs to the courageous? Man must act from out of his whole soul? Or should they tell them: if tomorrow you take something up with your whole soul, by midday you will no longer know what to do with it; but if you need that thing in the morning, without soul, for business, like the person from whom you stole it, you will still be in a condition to need it in the afternoon? — They probably will just give the stupidest answer that one can give; they will smile benevolently and say: you did something stupid.

2.

GLOSSES

GENERATIONS OF STYLES & STYLES OF GENERATIONS

When a young person visits famous cities for the first time, and sees Gothic and Baroque and all the rest of what he was apparently brought into the world to admire, he has the very distinct feeling that at bottom all of it has nothing to do with him. Not, by any means, because it is not beautiful; but beauty is obviously something very circumstantial, bound up with much that is superfluous, random, even grotesque. The young person mistrusts the raptures of adults about it no less than if they wished to convince him that mummy-schnitzel were really the ideal & most nourishing fare. He smells some sort of dishonesty, embarrassment, & palaver in it. It is, in fact, not at all the first reaction to find an old beauty beautiful; instead, the innate and natural reaction is to find it old. I don't hold it to be a paradox in the least to call in love as an analogy; a frank young person would never say of a beautiful fifty-five year old woman that her broad, restful forms & the filigree work of wrinkles in this admirable cathedral were beautiful. Instead the young person determines hastily that she is old, and probably will say nothing more, because young people take no notice of that which does not concern them. If one speaks with a gifted young Roman about cities, one can be sure that he will enthuse about America or Berlin, while Classical and Baroque Rome seem slatternly to him; he finds it a scandalous backwardness in street sanitation to leave behind rubble the size of palaces. In order to find one's way to art — I might even say in order to surrender to it — one must first have had one's soul repeatedly broken. If they had only themselves to rely upon, young people would build cities for themselves corresponding to their own world-feeling — expressing a sense of primordial resistance. And such cities would have to be very different from all the cities that already exist.

But naturally this task weighs heavily on their tongues and hands. Every artist knows how rarely it is possible to express an idea just as one means it, and it is a great deal harder to liberate the essential feelings of the ego from its inwardness. If one is not further away from these feelings at an advanced stage of life than at the beginning, one can wish oneself luck. And self-respecting young people are helpless; before them lies the vast expanse of thought. They don't even know how best to begin in order to come most swiftly into its depths. The aids proffered them by their upbringing and schooling have hardly touched them internally. It is therefore quite understandable that the young person runs after everything that seems like it might be able to loosen his tongue, to help him to his self-expression. It is this that produces the styles of the generations, which replace one another like fashions.

But it is more correct to speak of generations of styles rather than styles of generations. We have lived through this many times before. Every time a new generation appeared, it maintained it had a new soul, and declared it would now go about finding a fitting style for that new soul. But they did not have a new soul, only something like an eternal mollusk inside themselves, which did not fit into any shell; least of all the one that had just been formed. One can always see this ten years later. Around 1900, one could still believe that Naturalism, Impressionism, Decadence, and heroic immorality, were different aspects of one new soul; by 1910 one already knew (what only a few initiates understood, Alfred Kerr[11] had known even before) that this soul was a crevasse, & nothing was real about it but its sides. And today from out of this whole generation-soul there are only a few single souls left over, souls that the alphabetical categorization of Kürschner's [literature lexicon] or the catalog of the Crystal Palace can easily muddle together. There is evidence that the same thing will happen with Expressionism.

Kant said of the genius — in those days it was understood that he meant the artist — that he creates "exemplary" works, which are stimulating only for "posterity," not for imitation. The generation of styles is always this kind of spiritual emulation; not, to be sure, the sudden appearance of a new soul, but really the plunging & alighting of pigeons from all the rooftops whenever someone stands in an empty place and scatters fodder. Some sort of gesture, an external or an internal one, is discovered, some sort of technique, by virtue of which one slips oneself a simulated ego, an ego that lies between one's own nebulous self and the unsatisfying selves of the former generation. One is, for example, decadent, and everything flows splendidly and easily from this moment on; the biggest bruisers are able to lift more internally when they do it with a wearied smile. Today, on the other hand, in a period where lyricism is at the level of 'Oh — Harrumph!' even the weakling is happy with his syphilitic soul if it warbles in the jargon of a world-class weight-lifting club. Why that should be cannot be explained; it is a mystery. The people cannot find their personal individual soul and thus they adopt the next best more or less fitting group soul — that must be the whole mystery. Naturally one can call this fashion; but it is a fashion born of the deepest human need. There is plenty of swindle in it, but just the same there is always a small abyss nearby.

Put into one sentence: one becomes "stylish," but one does not miraculously give birth to a new style. Style is only ever made by the followers; when they run so far behind that they can't see the forefront, they become the leaders. Art history itself has, by the by, perpetrated no small calamity when it comes to this question, since it has called much more attention to the main styles than to the transitions, & thereby misled people to believe that styles are symbols of collective souls, which appear suddenly, in mysterious ways. Ever since, each generation of style searches for its style of generation. Really it is searching for itself. But just like a Münchhausen, who wanted to be pulled out of the water by his ponytail while simultaneously watching on the shore for himself to appear.

JOHANN STRAUSS AS A GIANT

Homeland art: that is the rallying cry of people for whom the pimple on their own face is nobler than the Monte Rosa[12] on Swiss soil. It exists in all nations. I don't endorse it, but that has not kept it from spreading out like a rash in all the colors of all countries. I therefore do not want to single out Vienna by questioning its right to have just erected a statue of Johann Strauss, despite the fact that, as far as I know, they still have no monument to Hebbel.[13] And yet, the accompanying unveiling celebrations were remarkable. When a newspaper writes: "Johann Strauss — is Vienna progressing, is the Vienna of work and creation, the source of the Ringstrasse, where the university rose to brilliance, where the parliament liberated the ghosts and the middle classes celebrated the triumph of their splendid public character...," I can more or less agree, since I am not entirely lacking in malice — although I never would have dared say so myself, that our local politics and scholarship do have a certain Johann Straussian flavor. When, however, altogether more room in the newspapers is given over to this great family celebration than all the other great artistic productions put together, when Strauss is counted as one of the most precious possessions of Vienna, for whom the highest veneration of Austria is "just high enough," and when it is stated in front of the Chief of State that there is a direct (presumably ascending) line leading from Mozart to Strauss, with Schubert and Beethoven as neighbors, one must simply and dryly, for the record, raise a voice of protest from the other Vienna, that part that has nothing to do with such tastelessness. More than this would be too much; or one would have to write a cultural history & presumably not just of Austria.

The offended monument-Komitatschis[14] will certainly count me as a supercilious curmudgeon when they hear that I myself hardly see much difference between waltzes and Negro dancing. Not even a difference between these two things and Eastern ice cream & Kugler bon-bons.[15] I would make monuments for the inventors of all of these. These artworks for the masses have an unbelievable emotional import; they unlock the soul, make us mindlessly happy, and are today perhaps the only symbols we have of universality and human communality. One could create wonderful monuments for them, touched by a soul's gentle irony toward its innards. One would have to explain it to the admiring recipients during the unveiling; although one should also be able to see it in the monuments. Otherwise, it will come to where it naturally comes, to a state of affairs where Anzengruber and Nestroy, both of whom I treasure very much, are thought of as great writers, which they are not in the least. Hallmer's Johann Strauss monument can survive flames, but not fireworks, especially because of its ardent surrounding figures. One approaches it in an innocent picnic mood & suddenly imagines oneself on the way to Emmaus.[16]

THE CRIMINAL LOVERS: THE STORY OF TWO UNHAPPY MARRIAGES

In the last few days a trial has come to an end in Berlin that has understandably captured the attention of many people and exposed problems that we can only wish people had attended to before they ended in a courtroom. A woman by the name of Mrs. Elli K. was condemned to four years in prison for the manslaughter of her husband; her girlfriend, Mrs. N., who was exonerated of the attempt to commit the same crime on her own husband, was condemned to a year and half of hard labor for aiding and abetting Mrs. K. The sentencing alone is remarkable; the abettor gets a shorter term, but a harsher kind of punishment. Who knows which emotional weight is heavier, that of the duration or the kind of punishment? And the psychological character of the act is, in fact, mirrored by this uncertainty.

Elli K., the daughter of simple people, married a master craftsman at a very young age and ran home to her parents after the first weeks of marriage, filled with a horror the cause of which remained hidden because the feeling of shame, even in this most critical situation, stopped her from revealing it. Reduced to a general surmise, one can only assume two reasons: either sexual brutality, probably accompanied by perversion on the part of the husband, or extreme sensitivity, caused by inversion, on the part of the young woman. At this point in a civilized society, especially one wherein we still ascribe so much importance to the family, the parents should have been in a position to step in with advice and help. Instead: the enraged father ordered his daughter to return immediately to her husband — the consequences of family authority, as is so often the case, in the wrong direction!

Elli K. returns and runs away again in a few months, this time to friends; she sues for divorce, but the suit must be withdrawn again because the plagued woman is still not capable of revealing the terrible things that were done to her or which she may have only imagined, aggravated perhaps by emotional abuse inflicted upon her in her parents' house, causing even a slight injury to be transformed into a severe emotional trauma. Thus the marriage of fear, disgust, and force continues.

Here comes the second twist, which, like the whole sequence, is as typical as if it were lifted from a scientific case study. Elli K. meets Frau N., who also lives in an unhappy marriage with a brutal man, whom she married after the war somewhat imprudently. A love affair develops between the two women; the probability that there is a strong lesbian component to Frau K.'s resistance to marriage is raised by this, but it need not be so.

A weak homosexual tendency, which is almost always present, can have first been awakened by the girlfriend. As is usually the case, the burning feeling is not satisfied by daily togetherness, and it is supplemented by an exchange of passionate letters, of which the court had six hundred on hand. It is decided that they would free themselves from their husbands & murder the monsters. Poison administered in unnoticeable daily doses is the chosen method. In any event, the girlfriend is the leader in this criminal relationship; that is already clear, because in the end, Elli K. completed the act, but she did not!

For, as experience tells us, in relationships between these sorts of couples, it is always the stronger one who does not do the deed, though she convinces the weaker one, who often refuses at first. The stronger one does not desist coldly, with the conscious intention of letting the weaker one do the deed alone, but the combined suggestion just works more powerfully upon the one who is psychically more susceptible. In this way, Elli K. becomes the victim of her girlfriend, N., but she commits the worse crime. The assessment of punishment always presents difficulties in such cases, & the investigations of the legal theorists who attempt to bring the solidity of the law into harmony with the brittleness of psychological decision-making are not always without their humor. Probably in the case of the two girlfriends, we can also assume a certain psychopathological inferiority, which must not necessarily be equated with a social one!

There is a book by the Italian psychologist Scipio Sighele, called *La Crime à deux* in the 1910 French translation, which contains hundreds of such cases, that almost all proceed along the same lines. As an example, I will give two excerpts from letters in this book written by a woman to a younger man whom she wanted to seduce into killing her husband: "Tuesday is the anniversary of the first month of our love; I am sending you a flower in remembrance; I will do everything that is in my power to belong to you alone [she had mixed poison into her husband's food!]. Oh! How I wish I were free! Is it really so difficult to obtain it [dynamite, that he was supposed to put in her husband's hunting rifle!]?" Another passage: "He was ill yesterday: I think that God has begun his work." One can gather from the emotional expression of this passage that not only had the noble feeling of love transformed itself into a crime, but that the external criminal feeling experienced itself internally to be indistinguishable from the noble feeling of love. With crimes of this sort one should ask oneself more than ever how much society is responsible for them, in that it lets things go so far. An energetic criminal may have more badness than a weak good person, but also more germs of goodness, said John Stuart Mill.[17]

MORAL INSTITUTIONS

The citizen is born with eyes, ears, a mouth, and a nose; in the age of majority he gains yet another organ, *a word of mouth*, or a reputation.[18] This organ is neither small nor large, neither beautiful nor ugly, but it is under surveillance by the police. And while one can do a good deal with one's regular mouth — pleasant and unpleasant things — one can do nothing at all with one's word of mouth. One has no power over it; that is the dangerous thing about it. Very few citizens suspect that their secret private life is more dangerous than a notorious criminal act, wherein one knows what one wants, how much one can be punished for it, and what the thing is called.

A not very rare case familiar to us all is the case of adultery. He who has not yet committed it, certainly has at least heard of it, for all the world is filled with jokes and comedies about it. But one can say, thank God, that people commit adultery much less than they talk about it, since four people can only commit two adulteries. One commits them quietly; but once in a while it happens that one party makes some noise, and in this case it is usually the party that is actually not supposed to know about it, and this party can make a denunciation, and, according to the laws of almost all civilized nations, the adulterers will be punished. When nations were not yet civilized, the punishment sometimes consisted of death; today it consists of maybe fourteen days arrest. This is not so much when one considers that the premeditated and successful effort needed to smash a window receives generally the same amount of punishment and is less pleasurable. Probably the law would like to be stricter even today, but marriage is a so-called holy entity (like, for example, art), and so the nation never knows how much it is worth.

What really sharpens the punishment then consists in something else, namely, in the *word of mouth* that is opened by such occasions; it is in just these kinds of situations that it emerges as a force that radically alters people. A case like this usually begins with a woman, grown somewhat strong-willed around the waist (with outraged tongue, flaming bosom, broken heart, and a corrupted sense of shame; in other words, doubtlessly already so terribly injured physically that she has a right to public support), dragging the "demonic woman" who has stolen her husband, the "seducer," in front of the judge, where the "snake" innocently defends herself on the grounds that everything that happened was only platonic. She can really say this innocently, since only the smallest number of women study Plato before they enter into a relationship with a man, and they understand by platonic merely a not-yet-entered-upon level of the unplatonic, requiring no particular study. At this point, however, the judge bids the organ of law & order open up the word of mouth concerning "the defendant's character," revealing evidence culled from the moral establishment; and the outcome for the defendant's character is, in all cases, annihilating. The former demon who was shrouded in mystery transforms herself into a citizen with a birth certificate and a residency permit, and she who just now was the beloved is revealed to be a "former cabaret actress." Yes, I knew of such a case, and it proceeded to a trial, even though there was no evidence, apparently only because the former cabaret actress had become the "owner of a coffeehouse," and had, after selling the coffeehouse, "pursued no orderly activities," but instead went on "errant adventures in establishments of pleasure" and especially was "on the lookout for well-situated gentlemen," whom she is said to have received in her apartment "even in the evenings." She was no orphan in need of protection; but did she deserve the dreadful verdict leveled by the moral institution in its annihilating report, concluding as it did with the full weight of an abused public agency, that despite everything it did *not* possess the authority at this time to take action against Mrs. X?

Here the foundations of personal morality collapse underneath us. Because such a thing can happen to anyone: no one is immune, however far he may stray, to the possibility that the moral establishment will have *no* authority to take action against him. Who among us has not once wanted to be an actor? And who would pursue an occupation if he were lucky enough to sell a coffeehouse? Who among us has not sometimes been on the lookout for errant adventures in houses of pleasure? Maybe even have received well-situated women by night? And if he is not a rascal, even well-situated men will have gone in and out of his apartment by the bright light of day, and thus he, or the moral institution, falls under suspicion of inverted feelings! One naturally believes that one oneself is a normal and possibly upstanding person, but therein precisely lies the mistake. One has only not yet given the moral establishment "the authority" to judge one. Lacking this, everyone is apparently on the same level. Man is only a gambler, whom fate lets win for a while, only to take everything away from him one day. For the eye of the law is watching you. You don't even know where its office is, and you can't deceive it. One day you will be slandered and never recognize yourself again.

This is why private life is the most dangerous thing that there is. It would be cruel if we did not suggest at least one protection against this danger. It consists in acquiring a public character as soon as possible, even if it is a humble one. For the eye of the law recognizes a public character, because it is itself of a public nature; and according to the old wisdom, the eye could not recognize light if it were not itself made of light matter.

Every civil servant has his own personnel folder, and if there is nothing specific about his personal character in it, at least he has his official character. But the most favorable documentary testimony about a private character consists in his not having a prior record and there not being anything else of a negative nature that can be alleged against him. And since, naturally, that amounts to the same thing as saying that up until now he has understood how to avoid the persecutions of the authorities through considerable guile, every private person can see for himself that, until he is captured, the state-controlled authority can see nothing more in a private person than a not-yet-captured criminal. The only possible exceptions to this are notorious wealth or a personal recommendation.

We have thought a good deal about the causes. They might be a consequence of original sin, for in the end it is this that is responsible for the fact that so many people are born without an official character. Things will improve as the peoples of Europe progress even further toward increased bureaucracy.

TWILIGHT OF WAR

Hungary pensioned sixty generals, but of those that remain there is still one general for every five hundred men. In Austria there were maneuvers this summer. Any of the 16,000 mercenaries that were present — no more applied for this job — who wanted to participate, had to pay their own traveling expenses. There were, at least, discounted tickets to the Salzkammergut, where the maneuvers were taking place. One read that the military spirit of the troops left nothing to be desired, and that the officers enhanced the charm of the Ischl esplanade. Polities like Austria and Hungary, whose budgets are well acquainted with a constant deficit, waste a huge amount of money that they do not have on their armies. That these armies are not maintained for an attack on their neighbors cannot be affirmed either in Vienna or in Pest with any great word of honor. But these armies are too weak for any sort of defense of the country against an enemy attack. Yet it is their existence alone that would legitimize the military nature of any incident. If Austria were to do away with its army, it would be more secure from the incidence of an incident of enemy troops than if it kept an army in readiness against one. Because in the latter case it would be a "military combatant." With good reason, and there are no other kinds, it could waive its military and martial capacity by dissolving its army and also provide an excellent model of disarmament, something people only ever talk about. The example could be contagious. Even Germany might catch it. If one wants peace, one has to do something, not just have a conference about it. There is no radical defense against war. Because there is no radical defense against the stupidity, fantasy, and bestiality of human beings. But there are a dozen small defenses, and none of them should remain untried. The weaker a person is, the more he will develop and pay attention to his intellectual powers, in order to carry on in difficult times. The stronger he is, the heavier his fist, the sooner he will surrender his reason in order to finish off a difficult thing with his fists. But that is not bravery. That is the obtuseness of brutality. Little David was brave, not the strong Goliath. He was nothing but strong, and he finished off nothing but himself.

No state has ever maintained of its army that it is kept for offensive purposes. Each one affirms that it is only there for defense. For four years dozens of armies have defended something against something else. Only one thing remained undefended, that there is nothing which armies could defend that could justify such an expenditure of human lives. It is a myth that disarmament would have to be agreed upon universally. Those who make the assertion want, at best, to just talk about it.

But this disarmament might only depend on one nation declaring on its own that it will refrain from keeping an army due to the complete pointlessness of defending itself against all the other armies in the world, should it occur to the rest of the world to attack it or to attack it precisely for the reason that this nation has no army, and is, then, more or less incapable of retribution. And thus, a more or less reasonable state is as likely to play the master in response to every nationalistic rowdiness as is a reasonable man in private life in response to a member of the student dueling corps who wants satisfaction in an "affair of honor." Why shouldn't a state say: I refuse to use poison gas, for I am not certain whether I myself will get out of it alive, and have therefore abstained from this sort of method? Let us tell the German bravura of a beer stein in one hand and a sword in the other, that there are many occasions to show courage, real courage. Without needing to rouse yourself to it with the Hohenfriedberger March, with flag-waving, drumrolls, liquor, newspaper articles, speeches, and fabricated news. One need not first intoxicate oneself on the blood of the enemy to find the courage for courage. It is only in song that one hears the claim that a soldier's life is a beautiful one — even though it can sometimes be more fun for a while than the life of a miner who, falling victim to the lure and affirmation of the song, throws away his pick and: Off to the horses, comrades, to the horses! Soon enough he finds himself in another hole with a gas mask on his face, whistling out of another hole altogether.

We should not leave any measure untried if it might postpone — as long as possible — the foolishness of making a decision based on the false justice of a war. Disarmament is one measure. Another one would be to exclude armaments from general technical developments. If this does not happen, then war in the future will consist of a few hundred airplanes with poison bombs against the civilian population of a country. It would thus be superfluous for the infantry army to train. A further means is to make war economically unprofitable, so that one can learn from the last wars that no one really gains from a war. In the case of a war, all factory owners, businesses, and all farm owners would have to declare themselves mere employees in their concerns and activities, receiving an income that matched their income during times of peace and that is not in the least increased by any war victories. War, with its grand national mandates is, first and foremost, and not only by the by, a business matter for all private economies. The expectation of doing even bigger business after the "victory" increases the exertions of the profiteers. That even a "victory" brings us nothing, but rather means loss, is something we learned from the last war, but it may not still be true for the next generation. Because no history proves anything about the future. These profiteers will always believe that this time they will pull the wool over the eyes of the besieged nation. The way things lie, there are countless other crude means — ones that avail themselves of material methods. One can expect more from these methods than from the moral means which the pacifists, who believe in a radical abolishment of war, recommend. These means dignify their good hearts, but much less their good rationality. The church & its moral power? In the Encyclical *Vehementer nos* of February 11, 1906, it reads: "it is an absolutely false, a most pernicious error to believe in the separation of the affairs of the state from those of the Church" — well and good. But the Church might do well to consider such affairs to be something other than the confessional school or the filling of philosophy professor chairs, things which are really negligible matters for a holy Church. They would do well, in remembrance of their great popes who left emperors waiting in the snow because they had committed crimes, not to seek cheap power in small things & easily won prestige, but rather in a deed worthy of their divine message.

After all, the sentence: "Thou shalt not kill," was not only adopted from the Mosaic Law because it just happened to be there and because one wanted to leave all of the Ten Commandments looking pretty together. But the number of believers who constitute the Church is too small for them to effectively express their moral weight against the war. The number of believers in the tightly clenched money bag is much larger than the number of those who throw a penny in the proffered collection box.

CIVILIZATION

During Poincaré's time, a French senator on the finance committee of the Chamber of Paris who oversaw the reports of the armament expenditure, was discovered to have been taking "percentages" from Poland & Romania. A few flakes from the shimmering armor had fallen into his pockets while he stood shoulder to shoulder.

I see this as a lovely example of European civilization. It amuses me that at that time Poincaré not only approved the loans suggested by this man, but also one for Yugoslavia as well. For that almost approaches rectitude and transparency once again. Every child knows that God is no longer on the side of the strongest battalion, but on the side of the big banks; but if the battalions are mere tools of the armament industry, then it is healthy to take percentages from them, and soon they will be trading them on the stock exchange.

The only thing standing in the way of all this is a leftover bit of European romanticism. The great nations would rather play the role of robbers than thieves; they clench their fists so they can hide their thieving fingers, and this must be accompanied by beautiful speeches. This is why one is so thankful for this senator, who has relinquished the robber pose in such an exemplary way and has let himself be unveiled as a regular thief just like a monument, without even slipping away from his post. An example such as this has to take hold. In Paris for example one is already today supposedly able to buy certain theater critics. Here one only has to be friends with them, which is often much more unpleasant. That doctors, legal counsel, priests, journalists, will only provide services to those who pay them, we consider self-evident; but when one wanted to win a senator, one had to (up until now; finally, change is in the air) do twenty people favors, so that the twentieth would recommend one to the altruistic man. I don't know if honesty is really the best policy, but it takes a long time, in any case, and is a convoluted currency.[19] And while here an antiquated barter system still prevails more or less, elsewhere the completely moral exchange of money seems to be in full swing.

Naturally one must not deceive oneself into believing that war and infamy could end if only these exchanges were conducted out in the open as fully and purely as in private. Dogs have excellent noses, but we people pass each other by without being able to recognize each other. When it comes to things that we want, our price fixing is still wholly unregulated and wild, and we are as difficult to find by the people who need us as a book is without a catalog. In the age of pure money, however, we will be transformed into numerical systems and we will be endlessly happy. Numbers that move by themselves, just as Pythagoras & Plato dreamed them.

AN EXAMPLE

We remember the Viennese Hochenegg affair, when, in a university lecture, the well-known clinician accused the medical profession of giving and taking commissions for the recommendation of patients needing special procedures or operations. Similar things are probably occurring in other places besides Vienna, and in the pure age of money such things will turn into virtues. For it is not only unjust but also thoughtless to demand that certain professions should forever be exempted from those market practices that have already been adopted by others. We have already given over our highest spiritual capital, art for example, to the commercial establishment, and want to make an exception only for a few professions that are necessary to life; and this is faintheartedness, for as long as one demands from doctors a different kind of honor than the general commercial one, one demonstrates little trust in the other aspects of life that have been dependent on money for a long time now. Here we must make a decision. Society demands the highest virtue of its most important servants: honesty. Even today we can still understand this, but, amid the liquid flexibility of the power of money, such a thing will become practically unfeasible.

Doubtless, it is not a comforting thought to know that one's appendix or tonsils have a commercial value, so to speak; in contrast to other consequences, one will no longer be quite at ease with these possessions; and it will make sense to see the family doctor as a competitor who disputes one's rights to them. For naturally one should not believe that someone could follow the call of his conscience and still take commissions. A person who takes commissions and to whom they are offered in different amounts will always let himself be influenced by them. But one may ask whether or not that definitively does more damage to the health of the patient. For a doctor who doesn't take commissions, who recommends a specialist or surgeon, would even today still be able to follow the voice of his conscience only if he has learned to hearken to it through exposure to literature or experience, doubtlessly thus only in a very small number of the cases with which he is faced. And in all other cases, his decision will depend on hearsay and other imponderables, including the voice of authority too. In the future, ponderable money will take the place of these imponderables, and one should not ignore the fact that there are accompanying advantages here.

So that we do not imperil professional ethics too severely, let us look at our health spas. The doctor has a very vague understanding of them, and they work for some patients & don't work for others. It is impossible for the doctor to finely differentiate between the effect of the springs and the rest of the facilities & in many cases he will base the more subtle diagnostic differences upon whether a patient would rather travel to the south or the north for either business or pleasure. Now let's imagine that the spas would compensate the referring doctor for every guest. From this point on, they would be in the same position as large firms who pay their agents commissions, and have we heard yet that bad automobiles or undrinkable wines have cornered the market because their agents received big commissions? The shameful period of uncertainty would be at an end, and the blessings of a healthy economy would rain down upon the doctor and patients alike. One could recommend a bad spa for a few years at the most, but no longer, because it would collapse as fast as a boring playhouse does, despite the best reviews. At the beginning more people would probably die than today, but in the long run more would be healthy, for the doctor can err, but the relationship between price, value, supply and demand regulate themselves according to an intrinsic law.

Nonsense? Or maybe even a utopia? By the way — since there are already so many specialists —, why not someday a specialist for the commission-free provision of specialists, who is paid & especially trained for this work? We hope, by the way, that all this is not nonsense, but really a utopia! Since, in the entire history of ideas, there has never been a utopia that turned out just the way it was planned. The same cannot be said, however, for a great deal of nonsense.

INTENSIVISM

Don't waste too much time on art! Find yourself without further ado on the pinnacle of expertise! All you need are two rules.

Always declare that a picture that doesn't please you or that you don't understand is old-fashioned. Don't include anything that will give away whether you have taken it to be second or twentieth century, a watercolor or a woodcut. For one can argue about those things.

Secondly, maintain, if people ask you the reasons for your judgment, that the painting style of the future is Intensivism. And if they ask you what this is, refuse to answer, and say: that's self-explanatory.

This is, after all, how it is always done. This is how Impressionism did it, and Expressionism. I will not tell you, of course, what these two words mean; happily, that no longer concerns you. And if I tell you a bit more about Intensivism, it is not with the intention of giving you an idea of it — because if the adherents of a movement had a clear conception of it, that would paralyze their momentum — but so that you can get a feeling about how this coming art will become the nerves, the will, & the vitality of painting. Stick to this resolution; forget everything else.

In the old days, people painted larger pictures than today. That was because their living areas were larger. You see how simple the rules of art are!

When we lived in castles, we covered whole walls with a single picture. Later, when we lived in houses, the pictures were 5×6½ feet at their largest. Today, even gigantic people can only afford apartments with a few rooms, rooms only half as high as they were before. And correspondingly the pictures have a format of only 3¼ feet. And if, as is to be expected, the building activity in Europe stagnates for much longer, the pictures will get even smaller.

But they have not become correspondingly less expensive. From this it follows that the ground and surface of the picture have gotten more expensive, the ground rent of the canvas per square inch has become larger, and the equivalent spiritual profit requires an intensivist economizing. That is the root of Intensivism.

Secondly, it demands psychic energy. Look at a landscape, and you will usually find a third, if not a half of the picture, covered with air or water. Such pictures are more or less fallow land. It cannot be contested that a quarter inch of painted blue or an explanatory note are quite sufficient to let us know whether sky or water was meant; every person knows what they look like; there is nothing new about it to depict; it is just a matter of habitual waste, a going through the motions. Naturally, you discover the same thing when you look at a portrait.

The painter does not fill the whole picture with it, but spares himself with a background, which fills at least half of it.

I could, for example, paint you two times, or you and then after you your rival while you step on his neck, the great day when all paper securities skyrocketed, or the black day when everything collapsed. Don't be afraid of such challenges; all truly original epochs of art came about quite naturally. Consider that one can paint many pictures inside each other. But I won't jump ahead; this art is already developing on its own. Just keep a firm hold on the wish that painting will soon turn to race horses, hunting scenes, automobiles, airplanes, and whatever else you find truly beautiful, and start by demanding that we put an end to all these underutilized spiritual surfaces.

Intensivistic life in the smallest portion of a picture, nervous surfaces, an introduction of the victorious energy of modern life into the frame of the picture: that is Intensivismus! If you see something that already seems to tend toward it, then say nothing more than: but is that ever intense! If this is too difficult for you, then always bring your wife along; she'll get it right.

SPEED IS WITCHERY

It is always good to use words as one should, that is, without thinking about it. One can easily go on for ten sentences before a word appears that needs to be thought about. This is doubtless a freewheeling kind of style that has about it an air of speeding traffic over a long distance. And it seems that the intellectual tasks of the day can only be mastered with its assistance. But if one pays attention to niggling details, one will go falling into a hole in language. Language no longer ambles along like it did in the days of our ancestors.

Consider for example the phrase, "head over heels"; what an important and much used phrase in a time that depends so much on tempo! How many people use this phrase in a rush without considering how many difficulties it creates for speed? For to catapult head over heels toward somewhere would be to generate such a frantic acceleration that your body would seem to be wheeling over your feet, & your feet over your head; speed grabs you by the cuffs of your pants; the law of inertia presses down on your head, and you are torn out of yourself like a rabbit out of its hide. But when was a person ever in such a mad rush? God yes, as a child, when one ran with unsteady legs. As a boy when one rode one's bike down a steep hill. Maybe as a horseman when one didn't really know how it would end. At a paltry speed of ten to twenty miles per hour! If a car or a train wanted to drive head over heels they would have to creep!

Head over heels does not express a speediness then, but rather a relationship between the quickness & the danger of the conveyance, or between the quickness and the excitement of extreme exertion. The streamers have to fly, the eyes have to lather, and the flanks must cramp. But then even a snail rushes along head over heels, in an utterly accelerated snail tempo, madcap, in peril. Secondary observations are once again always the decisive ones. It is said that a small car speeds faster than a large wagon, and the more worn down the rails are, the faster a train speeds. Even romping is a matter of habituation. There are neighbors who think it means carefully gliding along through life as if on waxed floors.

One looks around in language for more solid expressions. How would it sound, for example, if one said: "He stuck the dagger in her heart head over heels?" Even the most daring novelist wouldn't bring that over the lips of his quill. He doesn't know why. But he makes the dagger thrust like lightning. Quick like a thought would not quite be the correct speed for it. But a lover is with his beloved as quick as a thought and never suddenly like lightning. These are mysteries.

A general always advances in forced marches. Someone who has finally been found falls into your arms, but flies to your breast. A supervisor who comes too late blusters about; his office employee, on the other hand, enters breathless; the speed of movement has, for each of them, the opposite effect on their breath. Perhaps it also should be mentioned that one always comes flying, but is gone in a flash.

One can see that these are difficult problems. But the worst of it is that modern life is filled with new velocities for which we have no expressions. Remarkably, speeds are the most conservative expressions that exist. Despite the train, the airplane, revolutions per minute, slow motion, their outermost limitation is the same today as it was in the Stone Age; nothing in language has gotten any faster than a thought or lightning, or any slower than a snail. That is a devilish situation for a time period that has no time and that believes itself called upon to give the world a new speediness; the apples of alacrity are dangling in front of us, but we cannot seem to open our mouths.

But maybe the future will be totally different. Classically experienced speeds still do exist today, but only in places where one would least expect them: with farmers in the country. There lightning still flies through the air, the passing car blasts through the chickens, and there are paths where one can fall flat on one's face for rushing. In the city, the only speed one still senses is that of the connection that has to be made, the haste of disembarking and the uncertainty about getting somewhere at the right time. Without the blessings of neurasthenia, we would have already lost this kind of speed too, since in the worst case scenario, the person in a hurry, instead of wheezing and perspiring vapors, relinquishes a dollar and a half for a cab that will do this for him. And the higher one rises in the realms of power, the quieter it gets. A turbine factory with fifty thousand volts of horsepower hums almost silently, and the most monstrous speeds of technology are still only a gentle rocking. Life becomes more prosaic & practical the larger it gets. A boxing match between two professionals makes a lot less noise than a street fight between two amateurs, and an explosion is not as dramatic as a knifing. The great new intensities have something that our feelings cannot grasp, like rays of light for which an eye does not yet exist. But it will be some time yet before we really say relaxing-train instead of express, and only use the phrase head over heels when we want to describe or depict something like the evening stillness, when far & wide nothing stirs, and the rare quiet rushes over us like an ocean.

WHEN PAPA LEARNED TO PLAY TENNIS

When papa learned to play tennis, mama's dress reached to below her ankles. It consisted of a flaring skirt, a wide belt, and a blouse with a high narrow turned down collar as a sign of a propensity already beginning to liberate itself from the chains laid upon women. For papa also had this kind of collar on his tennis shirt, & it hampered his breathing. The two of them often wore heavy high brown leather shoes with inch-thick rubber soles; and whether mama had to wear a corset too, reaching up to her arm pits, or whether a shorter one was deemed satisfactory, was the burning question of the day. At that time, tennis was still an adventure, something today's coddled generation can no longer imagine. Oh, heart-warming early days, when one did not yet know that there was no grass growing on continental tennis courts! One fussed with the grass in vain, with the care of a hairdresser who tries all his tricks on his balding customer. But there were unexpected advantages to be gained on such natural courts during tournaments, if a ball fell into a molehill by accident or the opponent over a tuft of grass.

Sadly, they soon gave up these romantic tennis fields and created the modern hard court, which brought a serious streak into the game. The figures one might have seen at first disappeared, those who, aiming keenly, slammed their rackets with gymnastic dexterity against the flying ball; and the moves that are still used today — with a few exceptions, that only came later — were invented with surprising suddenness. Even the tricks of the game were soon all set & in place; but in those days they did not call them tactics and strategies, probably because they had too much respect for lieutenants and intellectual achievements. But that was really too modest: one is sometimes amazed at the genius of primitive people when one considers that they invented, practically out of nothing, fire, the wheel, the wedge, the canoe; and we, your parents, dear child, were likewise geniuses of tennis moves, even if I must admit that we were not thanked for it at the time, since one only appreciates such things later, in the mirror of history. But the spirit of the times creates its own tools. Great advancements in both average ability and first-rate performance followed after us, but we were the ones to give birth to the grace of this century, and for this reason, I am assuming the authority to say a few things about these matters.

But to keep to the subject of tennis for one more moment: ten years ago or less, one could still observe certain traces of the original morality in the sport. If one came from another sports arena to the tennis court, providing one had an observant eye for clothing, it was no different than having stepped out of a bright, open space into a forest of tall trees. Here the skirts still reached halfway down the calves & the bodice extended to sleeves that were close-fitting down to the wrist, while elsewhere clothing had long since shrunk down to the size of a sheaf of letter paper, if not to that of a theater ticket. Indeed, when it comes to the men, even today they still are, as is well known, totally sheathed in white, and it is only the ladies who shed garments from their arms and legs as we look on. This conservative aspect of tennis probably has something to do with the fact that, for a long time, it was a "society" sport, played for pleasure, and nakedness was not considered modern, but rather as a wardrobe secret that one only rarely wore, because it was always the same. And fencing, another society sport, remained conservative in the same way: this black silky art of the cavalier, which, when staged publically, seems to come more from the eighteenth century than the forms of the present, and thus lags far behind in terms of athletic rank. Fencing was a knightly sport and consequently not a sport at all, or it remains now somewhat like someone half-alive who, despite his lofty physical accomplishments, had to look on as the soul of his soul left him with the advent of boxers and jujitsu fighters.

A few things have changed, then, since the days when papa learned to play tennis, but it is more a question of *the value* we place on bodily exercise than the thing itself.

In those days, it is true, the connection between motorized technology and human cold-bloodedness did not yet exist, but the characteristic traits of true "physical fitness" were already established (with a few exceptions like golf or hockey, which one did not yet know about, or the technical design of equipment, which proceeded in a mostly consistent fashion). The "revolutionizing" changes in styles of techniques for riding, running, and jumping had already been made by that time, and even the crawl method in swimming, which was only imported later, differed less in its arm & breathing techniques from generally practiced speed swimming than speed swimming did from the leisurely abuse of the water in our grandfathers' day.

What made sports sports was thus not so much the body as the spirit. But before I begin to speak about this famous spirit, I have to tell a story that begins far from it but leads swiftly back. Everyone knows that Vienna is the second largest German city; but naturally it is much less well known by outsiders that a large portion of the inhabitants of Vienna live in Berlin, where they acquire large incomes in the particular northern German way, as writers, engineers, actors, and waiters, so that there are not always enough Viennese who remain at home. But because of this, we have hit upon an idea that is quite remarkable, not only for the nature of culture, but for that of sports as well: not only have we begun to build a giant olympic stadium in the last year, but we are sacrificing the last remaining piece of the Prater for this purpose. I must explain the significance of this. The Prater is one of the seven wonders of the world, which a Viennese person living abroad proceeds to enumerate when he gets homesick. The seven wonders are: the superior Viennese spring water, pastries, fried chicken, the blue Danube, vineyard taverns, Austrian music, and the Prater. Now, it is admittedly the case that if one says Schönberg to this Viennese, he associates the word with the post office W30 or the bus number 8. But when it comes to music he certainly only thinks of Johann Strauss or Léhar; and it is also true that the Danube is not blue, but rather clay brown, and that Viennese drinking water is extremely chalky; but with the Prater, for once, ideality and reality were in harmony. For it was once, yes, a natural park, wide enough for hours of wandering, right alongside the metropolis, with glorious old fields, bushes, and trees; a landscape wherein one felt, as a human being, like a guest merely — a surprise, for this nature was a good hundred years older than that nature whose face we normally glimpse. In short, it was one of those places that, if they still exist at all these days, are declared to be endangered and under protection. And this comes from some sort of sense that the benefit of shot-puts and driving cars is different from the benefit of moving slowly within an environment, yes, of sometimes even standing or sitting in nature, where feelings and thoughts are prompted in us that cannot easily be put into words. In the times when people wore full wigs they seemed to understand that. Although the Prater was a royal hunting ground in those days, where one only rode to hunt, there is much evidence that this did not go on without a feeling for nature. In the long tenure of Franz Joseph's residency, when our current way of life and fashions were first being developed, they were, at the least, reluctant to renovate, and only opened the margins to the public; the aristocratic jockey club & the horseracing club had to be satisfied with that. Only since we have been left to our own devices, and this is the most important part about it, has the Prater fallen almost completely to ruin, which will naturally not stop us from continuing to talk about it without noticing that it is no longer there. Where the Prater once was are sporting arenas of all sorts, surrounded by fences and entrance booths; and it could not have been otherwise, since one could have found places better suited for these things, but none so elegant, none of them constituting such victories over nature, none of them places where the ridiculous claim of physical fitness to be a renewal of humankind could be as ingenuously, as suavely, as instinctively expressed as it is in this context.

There is nothing that can be done to counter the fact that today we are living in a "culture" — of the body. But whose brainchild is this, really? At this point, I have to admit that I myself have played a good deal of sports.

Back in my youth, when I was home from school, I went to the tennis court every afternoon, to subject myself to a strict training regimen; or I would be hard at it with my *maestro di scherma* for a half an hour,[20] and in the evenings for another fifteen minutes, and finally the "skirmishes" with the major players, among whom some well-known fencers could be found. I participated in fencing and tennis tournaments, could stand on my hands, do flips into the water and on land, and almost drowned a number of times during swimming, rowing, and sailing expeditions. I think that this sufficiently proves that the spirit of the century was upon me early enough. But if I ask myself what was actually happening within me, I have to consider the answer with care: in the main it was probably really a blind force that drove me, some kind of inability to resist once I had become accustomed to it; but clearly this was mixed with that ignorant vanity of youth, which not only takes pleasure in its healthy body, but experiences a miraculous feeling, because all of the successes of the world are waiting for him in this magic sack, and no disappointments have come out of it yet. Neither should we forget the devotion one feels when learning about something the first time one gives oneself to it. If one has sacrificed a hundred hours and exertions, one will sacrifice the hundred & first too, and begin thus a new series: in this way, when one trains one's body, one is practically led on by the nose.

Along with these illusions, there is actually a wealth of rather minor mental qualities fostered by athletics that keep it from becoming a mere psychological illness. I will summarize these briefly, since they are trotted out often enough as it is: these are courage, endurance, calm, self-assurance. One acquires them on the playing field — not quite fit to be immediately used in all life situations, but rather as a tightrope walker learns how to balance on a rope strung only a yard off the ground. One learns to collect observations and to communicate them, like a man monitoring many spinning wheels at the same time. One is edified by observing the processes of one's own body, the time it takes to react, the enervation, the improvement, and the dysfunction of the coordinated movements; one is educated in the observation and analysis of simultaneous processes, quick intellectual combinations; one learns all the same things, if not to the same extent, that a juggler learns. One becomes familiar with the sort of blunders that occur before exhaustion is evident; one learns the peculiar balance between too much and too little exertion, which can both be damaging, the commonly unfavorable influence of emotions on achievement and, on the other hand, the almost miraculous nature of especially good outcomes, when the success seems to be there even before the exertion. And although one can learn all of this in other activities as well, like digging potatoes, for example, athletic activity gathers them all together in a thoroughly accessible &

attractive way. We can add to these the excitement that comes with competition, the besting, the back and forth between the opponents, the bluffing, and the belief in one's own success, and so many more things which are rather pompously called tactics & strategies of sports.

Consider the miracle of predicting the outcome of a race by which foot the runner springs off from! How complex would this single explanation be (though it can be adduced)! The essence of the self is illuminated from out of the darkness of the body by the sports experience, and a lot of other dark things are illuminated too. But I would really like to know how many sporty people today could be induced to even ask questions about such things or listen to such questions?! They don't need to! I have already allowed myself to speak about the triumph of sports over nature, and now I will trace its triumph over art for the same purpose, in that I will explain what will happen when the last tree in the Vienna Prater has become a member of a sports club. For artists' organizations have already made the remarkable suggestion that we chop these merely vegetating members down, and, for the time being, replace them with a "memorial grove." They call this "creative engineering" and justify it with the words: "In this case, art should not just be an art of exhibition, but shall work in the service of a paramount idea, namely, the renaissance of the body." Well, there is much that one could say about that. The crisis of the visual arts is great, & perhaps that justifies a good deal at the moment. But our society's inability to produce a nude that we could regard as an expression of ourselves is great too. For a generation we have dragged figurative sculpture over the barrel & under the steam hammer, but without success; and if the art that should be able to render us a human body can find nothing more beautiful or more profound to present than the bodies of athletic specialists or of athletes in general, then this is doubtless a great triumph of sports over spirit.

In the days of my naïve physical exertions I certainly would never have stumbled upon such ideas. I was almost through & through un-intellectual, only in order to be freshly intellectual the next day. While wrestling, little that was intellectual came to mind, and if I behaved like an animal, that was precisely what I wanted. Today I am still of the opinion that absent-mindedness is extremely healthy, if one has a mind. But under other circumstances, it can be very dangerous in the long run! But why carry on any longer about the spirit of the sportsman when the whole mystery lies in the fact that the spirit of sports has come into being not from its practice, but from the practice of watching it! For years, men in England have broken their bare fists in front of a small circle of amateurs. But this was not a sport until boxing gloves were invented, making it possible to extend this show for fifteen rounds and rendering it marketable. For centuries, short and long distance runners, jumpers, and riders presented themselves to view, but they were only "street performers" since their audience was not methodically regulated as "sports" spectators. Twenty-two men fight with the restraint of professionals around a soccer ball and a thousand men, most of whom have never touched such a ball, fall into a passion so that the players don't have to. This is how the spirit of sports is born. It is born from extensive sports journalism, from sports commissions, sports schools, sports academies, sports scholarship, from the fact that there are ministers of sports, that athletes are ennobled, that they receive the legion of honor, that they are always written about in the newspapers, and from the underlying fact that everyone participates in sports, with the exception of a very few who, for their part, refrain from practicing sports, yes, who are possibly even contemptuous of them. Provided one doesn't make money from it, one just gives in to it. One experiences a vacuum into which sports barges. One doesn't really know what it is that barges in, but everyone is talking about it, and so it must be something: and this is the way everything that is called a great boon comes to power.

But how unfair it is that we have not yet included the jugglers, the vaudeville entertainers — and the circus performers — into this culture.

And, above all: what a great moral problem is heralded in the coming age of sports by the marriage of business sense & physical agility in pickpockets!

TALKING STEEL

"Blech reden" (talking steel), an idiom meaning talking nonsense, is an ingeniously invented German phrase. It contains: the shimmering that is not gold; its thoroughly unpleasant sound; its boldness; something hammered out. If one were to say "writing steel," how many contemporary publications could be explained! But the use of this phrase is on the decline. Soon it will go the way of "eterne" and "troth." Later generations of writers will say in their commemorative speeches: "Our forefathers wrote steel," & an unbelievable shiver of veneration will come over the audience.

Why can't language hold on to such perfect constructions? When one finds a flattering word for anything that is hateful, one calls such dying the birth of the language. But why does language still live? It has become twice as long-winded as it was a few centuries ago, without correspondingly increasing its expressive ability. We leave out the articles, we leave out the verbs, we leave out the meanings; we step on its head in the front and on its tail in the back, but it is no use, language always gets longer. We are certain that it is becoming uglier, without being able to alter the fact. We complain about it, but obviously still persist in it. If anything can be called a dog's life it is the life of language!

I don't know too much about it, but people have occupied themselves seriously and scientifically with the question, and perhaps the results of these studies could be called evolutionary laws. Whenever one does not follow rules in other cases, one is imprisoned; but when one breaks a standard rule of language, one is honored as a founder of an evolutionary law; that is the difference, and it is not negligible. I recently attended a dog show, and I noticed a number of contestants who rather astonishingly fit the conception I have had my whole life of the word "mutt." In Austria we call a dog like this, who looks like a greyhound in the front and a dachshund in the back, like a bull dog on the right and a terrier on the left, a "promenade mixture." I asked around; they were in fact promenade mixtures; but their owners told me with pride that their breed had been settled a few dog generations ago, and since then they are called, if I am not mistaken, Austrian blends, have won many prizes, and look like a carefully normalized chaos. The human race is also this way evolutionarily speaking, as is the German language. Legal language, the language of the newspapers, of students, of crooks, of neighboring peoples, of the Catholic Church and the Roman Empire have, for better or for worse, left their traces; and if one does not want to object to the better, then why not at least object to the worse? Unfortunately, the well-known laws of evolution tell us that man restrains the worst least of all. But even language habits are habits;

and why is it that we develop bad habits with particular fondness? Language flows from out of the mouths of people and then back in, and moves from its point of egress back once again to the heart & nerves.

Because our fondness for bad habits is proof of a certain degree of respect for the contributions of mankind. One adopts such habits because by doing so one gains the floor. Because one impresses. Because they are in fashion. Because one sees and hears them every day. Because they are comfortable, and because one doesn't like to think about things oneself. But one probably adopts them most of all precisely because they are not good. We have a very humble suspicion when it comes to what is good: we have developed the idea that heaven is disembodied, alcohol-free, for non-smokers, and infinitely far away from us. We can only be partially certain that we have not acted artificially when we have behaved very badly. We suffer under the incomprehensibility of having once named something that we do not want to do, the good; and we do not feel ourselves called to proceed any further toward it than is absolutely necessary. It is very difficult to explain why we feel more secure when we don't lift ourselves up too high; we even say that the lie has short legs, in order to justify the fact that we love it!

In any case, it is true that in both writing and speaking we feel a strong aversion to the moral doctrine of grammar. But one especially ought to mention here that we do not even know how we might begin to put up a real resistance against this failing, nor why we should even do so. We need our language like the millipede needs its feet, which it should never think of for even a moment, if it is not to collapse on the spot. Happily, the meaning of words remains hidden from us. We all speak like the leader of the congregation, who says: "If we gaze upon this basis," or: "We will not allow the horizon upon which we stand to be ruptured!" One understands him well enough, even if he doesn't know what he is saying. How he manages that is his own problem, and the grammarians probably have no idea either. Apparently, the fundamental phenomenon of language consists in someone wanting to make someone notice something that he knows or feels quickly; to this end, there exists the most complicated system of cranks & levers that has ever made a person nervous; it is as puzzling as a piano, but if someone bangs on it with his fist, we know immediately more or less what he means, without even having to check where he was aiming.

So, one should not believe that something has to be correctly said to be correctly understood; and therein lies the mystery of a living language. It is horrid when one is forced, contrariwise, to be correct; and only bad writers make their reader pay attention to every one of their words. The reader notices immediately that in eighty out of a hundred cases he doesn't have the slightest idea why this particular word has been used, and he would be right to find such a mode of careful expression confusing. Especially cumbersome are the little words & the choice of their positions. But a good writer will always understand how to write so that one could rearrange all of his words and even replace them with others, without changing the meaning; this makes observation easy and corresponds to the modern principle of producing replacement parts that are readily available everywhere.

THE ART AND MORALITY OF THE CRAWL STROKE

 Dear Ferdi,

You seem, despite your nineteen years, to still be a novice, since you ask me whether the crawl is an art or a science. I have heard it emphatically affirmed by fourteen year-old boys that it is a science, and seventeen year-olds declared themselves quite certain that they are practicing an art. Doubting is not in fashion. But I will answer your question, as well as I can, and so cleverly that you will be able to take it up with the most distinguished of hydrocephalic patients:

> The paradox of crawling is: a á c & b á d, and despite that a + b ñ c + d. (In case you have resisted learning mathematics: á means smaller than, ñ means larger than). In words: your legs alone or your arms alone swim worse than usual in the crawl, despite the fact that you move much faster with your arms and legs together.

Why is this so? What physical or physiological processes create this kinetic contradiction? I will confess to you my shining hope to find, in this intermediary question, the basis for our striving after a decision in favor of art or science. In the "history" of swimming one can, at first glance, notice a rising increase of difficulty, and indeed, not because swimming itself became harder over the course of the introduction of different kinds of swimming strokes, but rather because comprehending what was learned became more difficult. The common breaststroke is, in its basic form, a very comprehensible one-way path directly through the water, not very different from the way one would move through every other mass. The Spanish swimming that followed after was similar to it in its leg movements; and even the wider, faster strokes of the arms (that conserved the breath despite the speed) could be grasped by reason. (You know? The arms moved like they did in the crawl, only they reached further out, landed more flatly on the water and were not only pulled against the body, but also crossed over it.) But soon enough the loosening of the leg lock, the scissoring even, that one sometimes saw (closing the legs slightly crossed), the rolling of many good "Spaniards," the stretching or gentle dipping of the body, were all hydrodynamic mysteries. Even when it came to the crawl, the simple mechanics of the sharp incline were no longer quite clear. It became necessary to analyze flow lines, turbulence, hydraulic gradients, slip resistance &

other plagues of the theory of solid body movement in water from the realm of ship, turbine, and airplane construction, before arriving at the self-evident realization that the sort of body with which humans have to do is not a solid one at all, but rather a resilient and variably moving one. All the same, it was at least possible in this way to gain a rough picture of the physical relationships that make the drive and propulsion possible in various techniques of swimming. And this alone could suffice to suggest certain tendencies in the development of this sport, even if it were not also true that an investigation of this kind would not be entirely lacking in charm.

It would be just as reasonable to consider a biomechanical perspective, based on the possibilities of the body's structure, which compared human swimming to that of animals. In the water we are four-footed. The natural attempts of a person who can't swim to hold himself above water have well-known similarities to that of a swimming dog, even more with that of an ape, as far as I can remember from a few observations made on such things. If one takes off from there, crawling seems like a return to nature, a cunning avoidance of swimming, that nevertheless substitutes all sorts of elements of motion that are copied from seals, sea lions, and master swimmers of the south. And betwixt and between, but separated off from this direct evolutionary line, we would place the breast stroke, as the original attempt to swim better than nature had intended, modeled upon some kind of rowing water animals, beetles, frogs, or their ilk.

I believe that such investigations could be quite fascinating, and, also, wanting to please you, and knowing that you want to take your sport "earnestly," I have tried to find some literature about it from the realms of physics and biology. I won't maintain that there aren't any, since I did not have enough time to exhaust all the possibilities; but one thing I can tell you, after utilizing the catalog & all the usual bibliographical aids in all of the largest technical libraries of Germany, not one single treatise on our subject turned up.

Thus, crawling seems not to be a science after all.

That is rather a bitter pill to swallow, for then it veers in the direction of art and personality. Truly, you did ask me right away what it could mean that crawling is practiced in a style, just like art, and where a phenomenon such as style even comes from. Naturally, you will have noticed yourself that all kinds of crawls — and this is by necessity — have certain characteristics in common, for example, the generally flat positioning of the body, the pliant extension of the legs, the webbed, foliated, and fly-swatter-like action of the feet. But opinions differ, on the other hand, about the number and scansion of the foot strokes in ratio to the arm tempo, on the form of the arms, on the degree of the body's extension, and above all, on the best synthesis of the parts. If one is forced by some circumstances or other to change one's teacher a number of times, one inevitably runs the risk of drowning. This is style. It will become just as clear if you have the opportunity to observe the phenomenon in famous swimmers: each one does everything in his own way. If you look at the swimmers' forms, you will find all sorts of variations, even within the same "leg" of a race, even though physique and achievement have some bearing on each other. Man and woman, each presenting, doubtless, different relationships to the water, do not, however, swim in any conspicuously different style. Yes, even the part played by the leg work, which looks the most mysterious, fills us with confusion once more, after long puzzlement, when we learn that even a man who is missing a foot can be the best of swimmers.

I would rather not answer your question then about what style is and means in a realm such as sports, which puts such strenuous demands on the spirit; indeed, I don't want to answer it at all. Only this much on the subject: one can only speak of style in achievements that are not explicitly made to order, where a certain arbitrary relationship between problem and solution reigns. It is a compromise to standardization, but not a careless one by any means. It is just that a method that is too polished, whether intentionally or not, always signals the end of a style; and such a method can only perfect itself until it reaches a point where it can no longer continue in its own way. This is what is meant when one says that beauty has styles; and fashions are closely related; but the essential thing here is not that the taste changes, but that it stays the same, namely in the form of something that never makes quite clear what it is seeking. We seem to have the remarkable characteristic, whenever we want something, of only wanting it until there is nothing left to desire; yet on the whole, we don't know what we should wish for. This is the way it is in art too, for the most part, where the styles blossom, grow densely together, and decay like the trees. And thus one can speak of styles of morality too, which betrays the fact that morality is not as much of a sure thing as it self-assuredly makes itself out to be.

If you try to apply this to doing the crawl, you will notice that even there the style consists in the art of alleviating a sense of uncertainty, in this case an uncertainty about the rational requirements of swimming, which can surely be cleared up soon enough by means of an equally simple process. Then style will only exist to the extent that different physical types call for different practices, & then maybe only in the way that each speedboat is always unique, despite the fact that it is built according to universally repeating formulas. In contrast to genuine combatant sports or horseback riding, where behavior toward another being comes into play, swimming makes few demands on the higher intellectual processes. But as I write the phrase higher intellectual processes, a warning is already burning on the tip of my tongue, which I have repressed up until now: On no account shall you look for what is high in sports — but never only for the low! Its value is misconstrued today & in a way that is so common that it is worth saying a few words about it.

We never hear anything but that sports inculcates humane traits, by which one generally understands that it instills in its devotees all sorts of virtues, such as frankness, tolerance, honesty, presence of mind, and clear & quick thinking. Now, this you know: the great athlete is not only a genius, but — as long as he doesn't take a kickback — also a saint. In truth, every other activity, taken as seriously, would instill the same virtues; & whatever other moral consequences sports produces add up to nothing more than an easy-going friendly state of mind and a self-consciousness about oneself that one also experiences as a sense of relaxation in the first days at a summer vacation home, and that familiar feeling for nature that expresses itself in the sensation that one could tear the trees from their roots. The fact that we look for the development of higher moral and intellectual activities in sports is a result of an outmoded psychological view that held that the animal was either a machine or, that when it sees a sausage, it must create a syllogism of the sort: that is a sausage, all sausages are delicious, thus I will eat this sausage. In truth, the animal is neither a machine, nor can it create syllogisms; nor does the human being, faced with tempting situations, conclude or judge in this way. Instead, what happens with animals and humans in quick operations is a layered synthesis of typical and personally established behaviors that "correspond" both practically and mechanically to external stimuli, and are simultaneously the function of an extended capacity for observation that prepares ahead of time, in the same way, that which will be needed in the next phase; and, finally, a thoroughly lasting, completely unconscious matching of the possible forms of reaction to what is needed at the moment: even a human being completes the most complicated actions without consciousness, without intellect, whence one can probably conclude that the intellect should not play a role in sports.

It is no humorless contradiction that there are very thorough investigations of such questions by philosophers and biologists, attempting to reconstruct the concept of human genius precisely by shoring it up with deeper research about animal nature, while our sports writers are still maintaining that the possession of moral and theoretical reason are self-explanatory prerequisites for the crawl & other sports.

3.

LITERARY FRAGMENTS

FROM OUT OF THE STYLIZED CENTURY (THE STREET)

Do you know what a street looks like? Yes?! Who told you that a street is only what you think it is? You can't imagine that it could be something different?

That comes from the two-times-two equals four logic. Yes, but two-times-two does make four! Certainly, we say, and no one concerns himself with the question any further.

But there are also things that do not owe their existence purely to an agreement among humans, and in such cases we cannot trust our logic so absolutely. Why trouble ourselves any further then? What I want to say to you doesn't require an introduction like this. It relies simply on a contradictory feeling: if you walk out onto the street you are suddenly among nothing but two-times-two-is-four people. Ask one of these people: "Excuse me, what is a street?" and you will receive the answer: "Street = street, period; please do not bother me any further." You shake your head: street = street? You reflect and observe your surroundings. After a little while you decide: "Aha, street, the people say, something straight, day-bright, serves as something to move forward on." And you suddenly feel a colossal sense of superiority, like a visionary among the blind. You say to yourself: I know quite certainly that a street is not something straight and day-bright, but can just as easily be many-branching, mysterious, and beset with riddles, with ditches & underground passageways, hidden dungeons and buried churches. You ask yourself why this occurs solely to you, but you simply let your thoughts cease, as these images enter your mind. You appease your inborn two-times-two logic with the thought that even this logic must preface everything with the comparative 'just as easily' if it is to be correct. And then you wonder why it is that the other people do not notice it at all. Perhaps they will arrive at it, for it wasn't clear to you yourself until this very day. And you consider further how all this might fit together. You can find no grounding, no matter what you may think about, until perhaps it occurs to you to look carefully inside yourself. You lay out a question of formal logic and your mind works on it with its usual certainty. So your mind is normal, & your mistrust turns, as is its wont, towards the puzzling mercurial part of your interior, which you sometimes call the emotions, sometimes the nerves, or sometimes something else.

You are terrified. You always are when something unfathomable begins to stir inside you; you are afraid, as if faced with an untamed animal. And yet you sense within yourself again, and even stronger than before, that sense of superiority. Your sleep that night was filled with a strange disquiet. Ghostly creatures came and went. Let us say women whom you had met during the day left behind certain complete impressions, each one self-contained. In your sleep, these whole emotions disintegrated into separate fragments, and each of the ghostly creatures had the combined essence of these partial emotions. When you awoke at dawn, you gripped your head, as if you had made a long frightening journey through places (degenerate dangers) from which no human being has ever safely returned?! Your entire philosophy of life & your ability to empathize were stricken from your mind.

During your morning coffee, with your back to the warm sun, you forgot all about it.

Now you remember it again. And in a completely different sense. It is as if you now knew precisely why a street looks so different to you than it does to the people whom you met. If before you were someone who saw clearly, you are now a seer. You see through things, you see them "to pieces." While the eyes of the others bring all appearances together under common concepts, according to their need for the measurable, your eyes disperse, dissolve, by virtue of their accumulated experiences, into the imponderable (slippage of thoughts), into the ungraspable. In everything you see beyond the forms in which they are disguised and sense the mysterious processes of a hidden existence. You are not inventing fairy tales, nor personifications; street remains street, house remains house, and person remains person; but you believe that you can understand and love all the things about people that terrify them like ghosts; and you rejoice about house and street, because you say to them: You hide all of this from the others, from the blind, all this which, because I understand it, raises me above them. Be thanked, quiet house! Along with the rustling trees in your garden, from your eternally monotonous melody, a terrible thought once flew, perchance, into the heart of mankind; quiet house whose nightly loneliness will perchance ripen one day into a thought, a thought that would suffocate from fear of its mother while still inside her body, so that both die of it; quiet house, while the strange creatures of my sleep may escape on new moon nights.

You look at all people mockingly and yet somewhat dreamily, as if you wanted to say: you are all really harmless conglomerations; but deep inside you your nerves are made of guncotton. Woe unto you if the shell breaks. But that can only happen in madness. Amid the crowd, you will become an apostle, a herald. You are overcome by an internal ecstasy, oh, yes, but without the foaming and convulsions of the ecstatic's spirit. You are a visionary! That which lies at the deepest edge of the spirit, that part of you through which the soul rushes in raging flight, when madness is already calling, which extinguishes everything in the next moment — this you see with clear eyes, still knowing that two-times-two makes four, & enjoying, vindicated, the colossal feeling of superiority over all other people and over that which you were yourself for so long.

You feel the religion of the religionless, the sorrow of those who have long ago sloughed off all sorrow, the art of those who smile when they hear the name art today — that feeling that is required by the finest people, who have already grown tired of everything!

Then you walk once more along the street, bent over and tired of it all. You know that one may not say: a street is a thing that.... But you have forgotten what it is. You remember that you once said: "something many-branched, mysterious, & beset with riddles, with ditches and underground passageways, hidden prisons and buried churches." — But you no longer know what to do with this. And an infinite hopelessness overcomes you!

CANNIBALS[21]

The sun had just risen above the steppe. Round and red. It was the enrapturing quarter of an hour, when the cold of the night dissipates and the heat of the day has not yet abruptly increased. The poet X[22] went for a walk. The sun shone down vertically upon the skin stretched over his temples, which was taut & embossed like the new leather of a club armchair or the good voluptuous binding of a heavy folio. Over his shoulders, the light ran like the oil of cocoa beans. His hands, however, when he lifted them while talking to himself, were almost transparent in this suffusing morning hour, & their polished palms shimmered like a faceted... gem in the most tender gradations from silver to pink. In the wide alley between the two rows of huts in the outlying city, children saluted his priestly headpiece. His limbs were covered by elaborately forged rings. His thoughts were occupied with a distich, because it was still held to be important to evoke a gentle overtone of spiritual shivers through the placement of a word. Had the slave handler not spoken to him, he would not have noticed his greeting.... Won't you buy something, sir, the animated one called to X... remaining standing. He was a lover of tender human flesh — it was still slightly surrounded by a frisson of mysticism, despite all habituation. And his career as a priest, which required that he determine the slaughtering days by prayers and inspirations from within, bound his interests to it all the more. Later, he said, I will come to you. What kind of people do you have...? Warriors from the upper Nile. Oh, their flesh is too firm; they are bellicose, muscular, and without nuance. If they are men and grown, sir. But the boys, if they are fattened up from childhood on, and the women too, if they don't work as they do at home and become fat, have an unreproducible aroma of strength and tenderness, of *rauque et douce*.... X continued on & thought about his distich and the great myths of his people, which he collected, and the wise & merry sayings, to which he sometimes added. On the way back he spoke to X; visited the copper smith, and X, the potter. He let them show him their new wares, and they spoke about the refined combination of abstract ornamentation and the surface effect of the pieces.

The prisoners whom he oversees are merry. They are kept in a good mood, so that they do not lose any flesh. X takes a few for himself, among them the sensible slave woman. His relationship to her is without eroticism. This sentimental European nuance is unknown in X. Perhaps in spring, when one sometimes hears the lioness off to the side of the hunting path, making different sounds, and when the jackals are restless along the great trading routes, something like that comes over the people too.

But one does it in harmony with these creatures, without looking for a human difference in it. Outside of war and hunting, the souls of the men are consumed by the great myths, by the thrill of the magical woods, and this is the backdrop of their lives. X takes the slave woman for himself, but he already oversees all of the fattening slaves of the city. Those that are not needed are sent on into the interior. It is a gentle occupation. It requires knowledge of men. The fattening slaves have to perform light field and housework, so that they do not become reflective, and they are retained for strumming, singing, and dancing, so that their flesh becomes tender. Only the unmanageable ones are overfed; but even in those cases, afterwards one tries to educate them spiritually so that milder methods can be used once more. Caring for them is a thoughtful occupation, & X loves it very much. One gains the wisdom of a shepherd. The men are allowed to have sexual relations with the women of the city; then the child belongs to the father and remains a fattening slave. Many mocking songs circulate about how the women love these fat mounts — especially the ones who were born into slavery. Such adultery is not considered a sin; it does not touch the honor of the free person, and the *corpus delicti* is eaten along with his progeny. Often, one of these slaves lives for years in the city.

One is satisfied; it is not an everyday sustenance, & nuance is required. When it is possible, one brings the flesh of a person of a certain age. They don't run away.

For one thing, a lone person who is unarmed cannot make it far along the great trade road anyway because of the wild animals, and secondly, he would only fall into the hands of another tribe. Thus they move around quite freely, imprisoned only by the futility of flight. They even circulate among the tribesmen quite casually and amicably. They live for their contentment, but it is really no different than when a factory boss jovially converses with his workers. One day, without their suspecting the moment in the least — for one acts in secret and with deception, in order not to harm their flesh — they suddenly receive a blow to the nape of the neck. Only some, who are needed for ceremonies, are killed with their own knowledge. In the first case, the difference compared to our life is only that our fate is not personified in a bourgeois fashion, & that we have no personal relations to it. (Naturally, also, that we live longer; but it is somewhat like the situation of a consumptive patient). This purely ideal and really inconsequential minus is countered by the great plus of a relation of tenderness, which follows from the requirements of the fattening culture. X really has an unbelievably tender relation with the slaves. It is a priestly profession. He often has the opportunity to reflect on and speak about these things in intercourse with Arab merchants, who execrate the practices, but as good traders they are not so recalcitrant in the discussion. He is interested in the slaves' lack of will. Even those who are slaughtered during festivals allow themselves to be led without resistance. It is a stupor of the will, an atrophy of the will because of their former lives; perhaps they also do not offer resistance because everything occurs in such a civilized and accustomed manner. One sees the well-known faces; it is a pleasant morning; the thought that something will happen cannot take root, remains abstract. — Possibly the fantasy of a physicist, or....

In a sanatorium in Switzerland, the high plateau of common sense.

Journal of Doctors: *Exitus*

Case study by doctors. Daughter of a factory owner?

[...]

Cannibals & Consumptive Story.[23]

Girl or young woman. In the first days after the onset, it is like a soft airy mountain bearing down upon her. Then the sun hails small arrows into her body. One feels: it is like the dry body of a violin. Fear: will she improve? Shame, to look the doctor in the face with the frightened question, as everyone does.

She notices her neighbor. He nods at her. She knows nothing about this man. Her husband has left her in the lurch. Even if he had no choice. She has begun the life of an outcast. A person — this man beside her — may be amiable; one doesn't have to know anything about him.

They help each other pass the time.

He had been a journalist. Traveled a great deal. Public franchises and publishing concerns. For the sake of success. How long ago that was.

They speak of the difficult condition of humanity. They come from the same country, are German.

He says: every combination of feelings is normal; it is only when looked at from the extreme development of one of the components that the extreme development of another person seems outrageous. One contains more possibilities than the normal condition of repose allows one to suppose [...].[24] And one has not taken advantage of them. — The woman had envied him, the traveler. If we take our environments away from ourselves, something amorphous remains.

Or he doesn't say that exactly, or only in part. And he tells her the story of the cannibals. Every night in the dark solarium. And they are "un-formed," step outside of themselves; they do not know whether they are telling this to each other or are experiencing it. It must be eerie; they are already living a different life; the whole world seems to have come under their power; these consumptives are stronger than the passionate creators of the world.

Then they are separated, since the woman's case improves, while his remains bad.

TRAVEL NOTES

Cacophony

A Visit to My Youth

Miniature view: visited Brünn, the city of my first years as a student, between seventeen & twenty. I enjoy it languorously, like a gourmand; everything is important to me that once touched my life here. Early afternoon rambling over the Franzensberg. For the first time: what a strange mountain. It bulges out like a snail's house in a spiraling slope; shrubbery, thin acacia trees. Have I ever seen a person pause in these places? They are only there to conceal these naked ugly flanks of earth that stretch from the top to the bottom of the city; one passes through them; the looping paths along the sides only serve to provide the illusion of a pleasurable walk; no one follows them; places that are not there to be pleasant, but to divert us from unpleasantness. (Symbol of our pleasures?) Humble mountain. Rocky paths, old broken balustrades, crooked lantern posts; on the benches, the muddy footprints of children's shoes; between the bushes, the scant loose earth. Above, an obelisk: from the obedient citizens to the good Kaiser Franz. Does one go to such extremes for the sake of pleasantness or in order to divert us from an unpleasant internal bleakness? Pathology of contemporary existence. A chain of associations begins with a guiding concept: ideals. The sun shines, sparrows chirp, not a person to be seen. Sparrows roister about a sycamore tree standing two thirds of the way up the mountain. One stands at the little wind-warped balustrade. Looks down on one side into the empty whores' district. Looks from the back into the houses like opened boxes. [...][25] In this city, it suddenly occurs to me, I heard Paderewski play Chopin for the first time.

Slanted little houses, angular courtyards with staircases climbing up the exterior walls, a hand pump, a saw horse, an overturned bucket. Everything in shadow. Only the little chimneys smoke away, and a cat, curled up on the ledge of a roof, lets itself be illuminated. Little forest houses, farmer-peacefulness. One night we went on a lark through these streets, actors & students. Broke into a little house like these. It had little square windows, petroleum lamps, sofa beds of black oilcloth. We didn't want anything. One of us stuck the tip of his cane into the vulva of one of the girls. We all stood around, she was a strong, ugly girl. The "mama" made a frightened face. Then the girl laughed. We all laughed. The mama laughed. (Was I there?) (Who were the others? No idea.) I don't remember any melodies. But I know precisely when a feeling first came to me. At that time when I was seventeen, when Paderewski played, it was bound up with the thought of a woman. This woman would have to be older than me. I did not see her before me; I only had a feeling about my affinity for her. In the arc of a minute; such a thing exists. And then I imagined really meaningless conversations with her, without periods or commas. Just so: as when one stands in the sun and is brushed shivery by the wind.

P.A. & THE DANCER[26]

A lady in the fourth row could not find a way to end her private conversation. A young gentleman behind her leaned forward and backward impatiently, and for a change of pace from left to right as well. But the dancer, who read aloud from "P.A.'s" books, had already spoken the word noble twelve times and the word exceptional eight times, when the lady thought of one more important thing to say and then finally became silent. After that there was a general moment of silence; then another inattentive mood rose slowly to the surface. Even the young man, who had listened with an amiable expression, became annoyed. She cannot recite, he thought. Then: she honors Peter Altenberg with ceremonial, formal German like a serving maid who has a fancy lover. Like a serving maid? — like a modest, good little serving girl, P.A. would say. Oh well. But then she danced. And she certainly did not perform a *Critique of Pure Reason* with her legs or the footnotes to Diel's *Den Fragmentis Veterorum Stoicorum &* her thighs did not elucidate the darkest spiritual uncertainties as Duncan's do. Instead, she danced more cabaret; she had a splendid costume, dulcet movements, & beautiful legs. Her legs sometimes appeared from behind her garments as the legs of performers appear in the opening underneath the curtain of a circus tent. Heart thumping. A fleeting scent. Loosened hair, green velvet, gold trim. But really the scent was the most powerful part, the scent. When one opened the trunk with mama's and sisters' winter clothes, the same scent arose along with the darkness that bedazzled one's eyes. One had to run away, lie down in it, steal something; one wanted to be a little stable boy or to go after this smell that receded into irreality like a growling gorilla with swinging arms. Only then could one make out the well-known friendly frills and skirts, perspiration shields and fur pieces.

Then the man's thoughts acquired a philosophical tumescence. Longing? What was it like? Sometimes I have longed for a glass of water, but when I really longed deep down for a beloved, I didn't want a real one. I did not suddenly see a new goal; I saw no goal at all, but I was saturated by a stronger, more masterful, foreign kind of expectation, like a room so radiant that one believes something must enter it. One feels a wonderfulness of receptivity, toward no real thing that exists, no real thing that one could receive.... The dancer slowly beckoned his memories into his limbs, like a hot lamp softly humming. The one with the scent and the thumping heart came from a circus in the city of Steyr in Upper Austria. Back then he was a little fellow and could not grasp that such wandering people could lead a regular family life;

and when the town dignitaries returned the greeting of the principals on the street and even remained standing with them, he was thrilled by their incomprehension. But in the meantime he had bored through to the unimaginable; in the back, in the make-shift walls of the circus, he had secretly cut a hole, and only when it let him see into the stable & not the dressing room did his courage fail him and he hadn't dared to make a second one. But then he rooted out a cave in the city woods and actually sat inside it, thought about the marvelously beautiful Blanche, who was below in the city at that time with loosened hair, in green velvet on her white horse, practicing jumps for the evening; and he fiercely gripped a deer antler in his pocket, ready for anything that might come.

But the next memory was from a restaurant called Casino in a medium-sized city. It was part of the cabaret, had little rooms decorated in white and gold, with red carpets. Habitués, regulars, took their dinners there, quiet, friendly, on their way out. But the fact that they stayed there to the last, gently and courtly, even taking the time to pause for a tender smile at their escorts in the doorway, was what drew him every week to this little Casino where he spent all his pocket money on a fine dinner that he devoured all by himself. How is it done? I want you: singer, dancer, trapeze artist... You already know how & what for. But listen, I don't mean to make any mere declarations of love; I don't want to throw myself away; I know how you are; I want to have you… with as little euphemism as possible, for you are wonderfully beautiful, dark… But don't think for a moment that I don't know how you are to be attained: one pays for a dinner, promises a jewel and says: *allons — allons* one says and already you know. — For an elite connoisseur, this is the only way that your beauty becomes the glorious abysm that it is. But how is it possible for one to smile tenderly without suddenly crying out from being in love & without begging you, despite everything, to just stay sweet…?

But not one of them understood him. They sat together, spoke of agents and venues, or read the ads in the trade papers. "A front man who can perform good somersaults sought." "Alto needed at 12 Sisters…" It is a profession, an honest profession. And if one accepts an invitation once in a while, why shouldn't one be really gay for once? That every night one has to say or do something indecent on the stage…, really, what do you have against it?... What can you be thinking? The people fly to such things as to sugar! Little man, even if somebody blames us, what do you want from us anyhow…?!

Then the young man's thoughts strayed again. As long as the widow is not thrown on the pyre, there are graduated differences. Whether one is the life partner of a new man every night, or for three, five, fifteen years? Or just being able to consider that it could be nice? And ourselves? When Kamilla A. dies or betrays us, we come down with peritonitis from heartache, and when Kamilla B. comes along, we are masters of shameless forgetfulness once again and in fact are actually truly pure and untouched. [With Kamilla M. we finally have arrived, and note only the mysticism of the experience; allow ourselves from then on to have our nails painted pink and our body hair removed in the Roman style; and we powder ourselves under the arms — all from an uneasy feeling of going astray and not being able to turn back anymore.][27]

When the dancer read something aloud again, the young man's earlier inconclusive thoughts about P.A. became very vivid. It occurred to him: P.A. was a great writer. But we must speak of a phenomenon that becomes increasingly clearer in this writer who has gradually been left behind: the more that he retreats from us, becomes less nuanced, more stereotyped, the more sharp his contour becomes, surrounded by a bright halo, like people in front of an evening sky. If we turn around, we see him like that on a distant chain of hills, walking back & forth, always here and there over the same distance, with an almost incomprehensible lack of weariness, but distinguished by that bright, bright halo. His heights are called the hills of goodness & are nineteen hundred and eight years closer, in any case, than the last ones of the same name. He will never leave them again, & manages a small apothecary there: Grillon's laxative to induce a soft, exhilarating stool; decoctions from the tree of life for little girls who have gotten into trouble; flowers for melancholics; little, primitive hourglasses for the all-too frolicsome ones. He heals the soul with a hundred genuflections and the body with encouragements; he calls this awakening the life energies. He is at his best when he is laughed at. If a girl says to him: "Be nice, Peter; the Baron wants to come to see Paula tonight; sleep for just this once in the servant's room," then Peter, like the wise, dear elephant, like the earnest, considerate tapir, follows the wonderfully beautiful, noble girl, and lays himself down on the servant's bed. "If it was a help to you," he says the next day to Paula. But if another one says, "Get lost, Peter! You're a dishrag, not a man!"— he gathers up his soft organs, lifts up his eyes to her once more, and leaves. Leaves and soon stumbles again over his soul's intestines, drags them along, hears laughter, gathers them up into himself again with a patient gesture, and continues on. Continues nobly, sad & ridiculous, legendary, and with a face quite similar to our own, ... a Christ with a pince-nez of horn.

This occurred to the young man about the remarkable and beloved P. A. while he wandered through his writings. Why? He didn't know. It would have been much more tender if he had not had all of that other business weighing on him. For which reason he finally became terribly out of sorts, and devoted himself, somewhat sadly, to the little dancer all the more.

But now, not only because she danced wonderfully, but also because she read so poorly and made P. A. small with her anxious efforts. A languorous longing rose in the air. This longing, he felt, is like the half-illuminated circus when one comes too early for the show. Blanche will appear, Blanche will smile, Blanche will accept the invitation of the Herr District Commissioner. She will be laid down at night in the great empty circus, where only a gas-lit star burns; and when one opens the door she will smell enchanted, like the clothes in mama's chest. And even at home, when he looked at the room in which he sat in the mirror and found it a bit unreal, he said to himself: one ought to follow that trail more often... feelings that have never become real, sudden, reckless flashes.... What was that like back then... and even an hour ago? One ought not forget such things immediately... Then he thought of how he had seen Blanche one more time; it was the only kiss that she had ever given him, on the way to the train station in Leoben; he had been fifteen years old; Blanche was already somewhat gaunt in the face. "We are going away tomorrow, away from Europe," she said, "to Spain..."

SUMMER IN THE CITY

I couldn't decide whether or not to leave town at all. In between two or three rainy days there always comes a half-summery one where the puddles stay in the sky and the sun swims in a friendly way between them. I drift around the city; there isn't even enough cosmic energy for a trip to the suburbs in this air that is cold and enervated by the rain. I float along the narrow crestfallen streets of the inner city like a gondola. Somebody calls to me. Slowly in passing he laps at the edge of consciousness, establishes himself; I stand, reflect for a long time... Human sorrow can collect in the worn-out knees of a pair of pants. His face looked like a cornfield cut with a sickle. We used to go to school together; after graduation he suddenly became an actor. I only learned about it much later. Nothing had even suggested it. He had been a sober, dependable fellow, and even at the time when we all wrote poetry, he had taken Uhland as his master, and wrote very reasonably constructed ballads. I thought at the time that there had always been something American about him, something in the way of being a servant and editor, lawyer and train conductor, teahouse manager and preacher in succession. But since then he had been a director more than twice, once the manager of a small provincial theater, and had always been an actor at the same time. He had been married while he was still young & had been doing well; and during the whole time, God knows why, he had not cheated on his wife one single time. Now that he was divorced he had no money with which to make up for lost time & his hair had already begun to fall out. And I, I said, "My God, these times are not suited to high quality work." "I have read your books," he answered. "When I was a director in Reichenhall. They are not quite the thing." — I felt that he was not expecting an answer; yes, that he wasn't even talking about my books, but about something else that was unknown to me. And so I simply said, "Yes, yes," and after a while: "You are young, well preserved, free; you are living life to the fullest here & have a very reasonable contempt for all books." "Life? Pshaw," he blurted out to a passing woman — . "This vulgar life, what do you get from it? And besides, I have no money. What? So? She would merely take half of my last kreutzer from me, & inexhaustibly, like a harpy... they suck one dry & give no thing back, nothing, nothing, nothing. I have my ideals." I didn't understand at first. "I have them, you see, have, have them, like one has a hat, a scrap of money, a ticket for the tram." "Perhaps you haven't eaten for too long" I suggested with concern, "one can't carry ideals in one's pocket, you know." "Posters," he blurted out, and looked around to check if there were any to see...

"I have retrieved the immediate burning possession of my feelings again, the way one has them in childhood. Come with me tomorrow." I had no idea what he meant, yet I had the strange feeling that I did understand him. I said: "You collect? ... Poster art?" But I knew that this wasn't it. I had a lot of time to reflect, and before the following day a remarkable memory came to me. My uncle Hermann once told me, when I was a boy, that his horse was sick. Give him to me, I begged, if he is sick. And he answered, laughing, the good silly uncle, yes, when he croaks. I didn't know what 'croaks' meant, and thought that it was some common occurrence in a horse's life. I had asked him with a tentative, sassy desire, motivated by something or other in his tale, really convinced of the impossibility; and all of a sudden a stream of blood rushed from the ground up to my hair, an overwhelming happiness, an intoxication, that neither danced, nor laughed, but rooted me to the earth with its overwhelmingness. No woman could induce such a feeling. Until my good uncle explained what croaked meant. Another time — cut-out lions — and the third time it was a cardboard horse on a box of bon-bons.[28] — Later still, I experienced real horses with a shimmer of that feeling. So I was not astonished the next day when my friend, when we met, greeted me with the words: "Did you say two-dimensional art? Art? Not that. Art is the ultimate aberration. — You go to the outskirts without finding much." — My family was in the country;

my friends were in the country. No one in the city knew me. I was ashamed to look for posters with my friend, yet it lured me like a secret. It was an event. The poster is naïve? Indeed. But try for a moment to take it totally seriously for once, more or less literally. It is not naïve at all, but grasps one deep in one's soul. The pickings were deemed bad by him. In a common tavern he pulls out some tarot cards and begins to play. I resist. Now he plays his highest card: the Prater amusement park.

SHADOW PLAY IN THE LITTLE CITY

Every morning at half nine the district doctor said the same thing: "If someone comes calling for me, you know where I am!" After he said that, the good fat mare stopped in front of the front door with the light-weight country wagon. Its four wheels stood very close together because, aside from a narrow front bench, they only carried two seats and a half-shell shaped canopy, that was clapped shut in good weather but which, if it rained, smelled comfortably like old leather. Frau Magdalene Steiner never said anything in response to his statement, which was half a question, half an affirmation. She stood atop the little flight of stairs that led from the house's foyer to the street, held her arms still, crossed over her stomach, without moving a muscle. She was just there for the sake of order, as her husband laid the equipage & his raincoat on the empty seat, clasped the leather storm coverlet over his legs, and took the reins from the stable boy from the inn where the horse and wagon were kept. As Dr. Steiner slackened his hold and then eagerly jerked on the reins, the mare was set in motion, and his farewell glance landed on the steps like a little stone that one throws over one's shoulder; Frau Magdalene winked & smiled after him in a way that would be difficult to describe, but that encompassed twelve years of marriage and the children. The only thing that displeased her about their life was that the narrow foyer led from the front door back to a staircase that led to the upper story, which was inhabited by another party, so that their apartment, which lay on either side of this hallway, was bored through like an apple by a worm. It was always pleasing to talk with her husband about how much their own house would cost, about how much savings they might already have available for this purpose, & how the savings could be used as mortgage. But the progresses of science require sacrifices too; an x-ray chamber had been constructed a short time ago, which even the district hospital did not possess; and the purchase of a little automobile, the like of which all thoroughly modern country doctors have, could hardly be put off for much longer. Perhaps one could procure a used one; nevertheless, under these circumstances, even with the most careful accounting, it could not be expected that they would move to the house before their youngest left school. But this time was resolutely foreseen, and the husband and wife really had no other troubles. At three in the afternoon the office hours began; her husband was usually back by then and had already eaten. When the office hours were finished every day, Frau Steiner shook her head a few times, and on rainy days she sighed, while her eyes assessed the floors in the foyer and waiting room, for the farmers tramped so much dirt in on their shoes. From time to time she imagined, darkly and vaguely, what a picture of an elegant city practice would look like, while her young maid swept and mopped the floor; but usually she thought nothing at all, but just stood tall and watched, making a reproachful remark about the bad manners of the farmers, so that the maid, feeling flattered, sat up on her knees and repeated the same thing. Then they briskly put everything in order, one of them motionless and observing, her arms crossed over her stomach, the other speedily, but both of them taking part in something important and legitimate, for a great deal of the earnings came from these dirty foot prints.... During this time her husband was in the hospital or with the few patients of the little city. There was a bowling night, and plenty of other entertainments. They kept pace with the times, not exactly fast, more like this: one stands with arms crossed over the stomach, observes the times, and follows with a barely perceptible movement out of the corner of one's eye; if they slip away, one goes more quickly for a few steps to catch up. One thinks with a measure of contempt, and quietly. One has strong principles, because otherwise the inertia of life would be unbearable. But this is how she gets her halo. Herr Steiner doesn't need to ask Frau Steiner whether she knows where he is to be found. She received the messengers and took the telephone orders, and she knew the roads as well as his brown mare. Even if one doesn't go on country outings, if one was born in the middle of the country, still, once in one's life, at Whitsuntide, Easter, for a birthday or name day, one went somewhere; and before one is twenty years old, one has been everywhere. After supper, he read the medical journals or the newspaper, and yawned. Then the conversation turned to the house & the mortgage. Or to the happenings in the little city. Herr Steiner would tell her about an interesting case in his practice. Or he knew, since he is also the legal and police doctor, about the latest murders or thefts in the neighborhood. But he himself is not overly fond of psychologizing. If it isn't a matter of idiots or insensibly drunk people, he thinks that they should have been able to understand the injustice of their acts, and that they were not completely hindered from a free (decent) use of their will power. But since the contemporary tendency in medicine is to make all kinds of concessions and nonsense, he prefers to pass off all such cases to the main county seat. But if he has nothing at all to report and it is not yet half ten, he tells stories about the war. They had married shortly after it ended. And, of war, if one has fought in one, there is naturally quite a bit to tell. One has seen many famous persons with one's own eyes, not to mention the dangers and adventures. One doesn't need any particular cleverness to live, just manners, character. In summer the city people come to us, but if they only knew how beautiful it is in winter!

— That is how the young people speak. It is ridiculous to believe that this life is more paltry than in the big cities. It lasts twice as long & weighs twice as much. The cheeks that were like an apple later become over-red like an autumn apple, and finally like an apple in the winter, with many wrinkles, but a good exotic taste. Only one must not have any imagination. People who remain happy under these circumstances have had their imagination removed by a good fairy in their cradles.

One day the rumor circulated in the city that at the castle Trauneck, the owner, Baron —, had been murdered, and by evening the rumor was confirmed. In an out-of-the way empty granary the maid had found the corpse, downed by one shot to the face, and in the warm spring weather it had already begun to rot terribly; the Baron's own gun and a spent shell lay beside him. At first one suspected suicide or an accident. But there are observations, each of which is so minute that no one wants to report them; still, there are so many of them & they are so mysteriously connected that an allegation begins to spread from mouth to mouth, which no one believes in yet, although every one adds a little to it. Thus from the start, the story was told among the servants that he was killed by a stranger — no more certain at first than the disquiet that grips livestock before a storm, but by evening the criminal commission had also found evidence that pointed in this direction. The next morning one heard in the city that suspicion fell on some foreign workers who were renovating the castle. That was very easy to understand, but already by lunchtime one heard that the workers had proven their innocence absolutely. They were completely in the dark. And the arrests of vagrants and foreign migrants made by the country police proved equally untenable. The Baron had only wanted to stay two days on his estate in order to oversee the work; but he had stayed three; on the evening of the third he was murdered. A telegram from the Baroness who had been concerned about his absence was found in his wallet. The wallet had been ransacked, as were the pockets of his clothes, but apparently nothing was missing, and the murderer must have been deranged. The Baron was a quiet man in his fifties; each year he spent a few weeks on his estate, to hunt and to see to the farm. His forester and his steward were familiar figures, and once or twice a year the high-ranking citizens of the district were called to a great hunt. Thus had his father lived as well. One did not know very much about this family, who must have arrived once from far away; certainly they had been a foreign outpost at Trauneck for more than a hundred years. After having once established itself here, the outpost had been overgrown with local moss; one didn't bother oneself about them and considered them part of the pride of the area. The area really consisted of nothing but these staunch centers. No, the doctor doesn't really need to ask his wife if she knows where he is going: there was the farmer in the woods, Mr. Moosleitner, the Fox Estate, the Ebenerding train station, the hamlet of Pösting, and the mill in Siergraben; she had only been there once, herself, but these things always remained in their place, as far as one could imagine. It was thus no different than if a beast of prey had broken into the region's sense of peace. Every report that this or that clue had to be abandoned was like the news of a new horror. One spoke of little else; at the least one contributed speculations about the investigation, and gradually an utterly improbable suspicion arose. No one had wanted to say it straight out, and if asked, would have insisted that something like that was totally senseless. But thus is a poem, too, created out of words that seem to have nothing in common; and in that sort of intoxication, everyone made a poem of the same suspicion.

WAR DIARY OF A FLEA

Preface

Such faithful companions as we are to mankind — our claim to this title is much greater than that of the dog, since on the whole humans have many more fleas than they have dogs, even if only because multiple fleas alight on each dog — and as significant as our contributions to the development of humanity have been, since the fear of us has added so much to their cleanliness, and the use of soap is well known to be a measure of civilization: despite all of this, humans have spread many imprecise ideas about us. They even know nothing about our life expectancy. [...][29]

I know that my race does not occupy a comfortable position in the age of hygiene. — The poetry of fleas is utterly old fashioned. — But as long as books are written about fleas & dogs... Moreover, nobody will deny that we are extremely bellicose and brave. We may lay claim to our place in the age of militarism as much as in the age of sports. Supplement: I was taking my summer vacation with a Tirolean farmer... on foreign ground. Parasite of blood. What a symbol!

And I believe that most people think of us as seasonal animals, like mosquitos. Indeed, the mortality rate for us fleas is horrifically high, but only because we are subjected to the most gruesome persecution & rarely die a natural death. But I can assert, and regard the contrary evidence of science without concern, that the natural life span of a flea is not really so short at all. In 1914 I was already a flea in the full ripeness of my intellectual capacities, and today I am writing my memoirs; my memory is excellent and I feel as of yet none of the bitterness of aging which Casanova felt while writing his.

A second prejudice has to do with our irritating nature. Here I must admit that there are of course wholly ordinary fleas; yes, that perhaps the majority of us deserve the scathing judgment which people are always ready to wield against us. In my opinion, however, these characteristics are only a result of our long history of cohabitation with mankind. We are hard-nosed, athletically skilled, death-defying, not to be shaken off; once we have set our minds to something, we sacrifice the blood of other creatures, and multiply in great numbers since we treasure love & family highly: these are characteristics of the strong man, which, however, he never grants others the right to possess.

If, nevertheless, I speak of a prejudice, I really mean that one must differentiate between fleas just as much as one must do so between people. Those caught by man are the intrusive fleas, while the intellectual, sensitive, educated, delicate fleas elude his acquaintance — aside from which, it would be an unjust requirement if one demanded of fleas that in their case alone the highly refined creatures among them would make up the majority. One will make the acquaintance of such a flea in me, and I can thus dispense with a description except for one preliminary remark: a fine flea puts great value on cohabitating with an important human. He searches for a long time until he finds the one who attracts him; and then he is not easily parted from his companion in whose intellectual & physical destiny he takes a lively interest. He strives to spare him all possible unpleasantness in their shared household, and nourishes himself therefore from people — or animals — with whom they come in contact, & goes on hunting expeditions from which he returns as quickly as possible. In this he has — I must mention this so that what comes later will be understood — a talent for orientation like a migratory bird. And only in emergencies does he assault the gentleman or lady in question. Once in the course of many months the city dweller notices with annoyance — in the solitude of rural nature it happens much more frequently — that in his car, on the streetcar, in the train, in a crowd, or through the cursed dogs who turn the house into a pig sty, he has been visited by a flea: of course, it is commonly the case that this is the vulgar flea (Latin: *pulex irritans*); but sometimes the human has no idea that it is the same extremely discreet spiritual flea who has lived with him for years.

It is indeed true that we are born in filth. But not a few upwardly mobile people are proud of precisely that in themselves. And in general, the human process of giving birth, as well as much else about and within human life, is not exactly the cleanest. It is not true that we prefer badly groomed humans. Ordinary fleas probably tend toward this just as often as ordinary people do. The fine flea loves clean skin and aromatic linen. During my life I have frequently mingled in the highest circles of society. The only thing that gives me license to bite is my intellectual superiority, a kind of fury toward successful people. Never have I hurt a genius.

A fine flea naturally understands the language of humans. It is well known that the opposite is never the case. Understandably, since persecution spurs the intelligence on. That is also the reason why a cultural flea has never yet been caught. Outbursts of angry words betray the murderous intent to him and give him the chance to hide himself in time. That which has been caught between human fingers has always been only a common flea who had not learned the language. I will not conceal the fact that the death of such crude creatures leaves me cold. On the contrary, the more of them that are killed, the better! I have no nationalistic feelings!

It is very unpleasant for him that he is a flea, although also a great writer… Later conversations with the sword, with the fly.

Beginning: Rome and Porto d'Anzio. Pension Kaiser & Wacker. In those days I had my perspective: on top of Madame Parmentier's knee.

Difficult existence because of the shamelessness of the Italian fleas. Conversations. The beautiful Ottavina. The good houseboy. In Porto d'Anzio. The aircraft-lieutenant and my gentleman as rivals.

Moonlit night in a remote part of the beach. Madame Parmentier sits; Madame Parmentier even allows her skirts to be raised and her knees to be admired. There, a sound. Quickly they stash everything suspicious. The lieutenant. Simultaneous pistol shots by the sea.

The next day, the first serious reports. Everyone still optimistic. My master earnest. Madame Parmentier is of no more interest to him. It is time for me to leave my post if I don't want to remain behind. My master seems to be in love with a Professor from Württemberg.

Departure. Arrival in Berlin. As after Sylt. Long stay in a station. The regiment passing through (as on Sylt). Difficulty proceeding. Graveyard earnestness in Berlin. The crush at the Austrian consulate. The Mobilization. Great times for fleas. Our historic preference for straw. We must wait for answers. The mystical. Quartermaster Stein & the victories in Belgium. Kerr, Bei, etc.[30]

He makes his way to his steady master only after detours. Shortly before the moment when he is wounded. Just then upset about the Austrian weapons and their insufficient reach, and Austrian politics as the cause.

Has an impulse to flee, which is, however, overwhelmed by the push forward. Receives the blow — lets out a small sound. Satisfied about being wounded. Then fear while lying there. Also describe something of the satisfaction a spiritual person enjoys in the distinction of bravery, although he is honest with himself. Story of the battalion fund. Excursion to Landtmann and history of the altar door.[31] Then these half dangers, which are like dangerous swamps, waiting, uncertain, strangely attractive. The resonating shots here and there in the mountains (throwing stones, little grey)[32] belong here, warped danger. — The experiences with Hradezny[33] & Vidale[34] (he was named something like Rhadetzky and was shot through his backside).

[...][35]

"Flea" (War Diary and Life Story of a...) (Experiences and Thoughts.) The figure of the waiter at the Army High Command. (Waiter from the Thalhof). He manages everything in his discreet, independent way for everyone and enjoys their trust. The flea has chosen him as a permanent post, but nourishes himself as much as possible on orderlies and unpopular persons. Only rarely, as a special delicacy, does he resort to a favorite. For he knows that he is unpopular, a vermin, a parasite. He has come far enough to see it himself. He bears the burden of the history of his people. Although his ancient, widely educated race is capable of wondrous achievements. In sentimental hours it sickens him that he is a nomad. But when it comes to blood and soil, he has a heroic connection to blood. He is an expert in blood. It saddens him that he is a bother to everyone. He hates the lice, the untalented parasites, who spread during the war. He is aware that his people are being exterminated: he is an individualist. Melancholy: ironic agreement that "progress" is bound up with a war against his people. Mussolini ousts the fleas from Italy. Even their old domicile in Turkey is contested. In his youth he was in an institute and perched himself upon an orderly or on a maid; he knows the current dictators from their days as students.

He himself laments in the introduction that the hero of his memoirs is a flea. But every time has its memoirs, and he is a lonely individualist. (I am a German flea. I have a deep relationship to German blood. And I am a flea in your ear.)

THE TOADY

In six days God created the heavens and the earth. On the seventh day he created nothing. He simply was pleased with everything. And yet, on this day, a creature came into being. This creature was the toady. He was made of pleasingness.

If it be the Good Lord's will to consider whether I might be created entirely out of nothing, began the little toady — yet I commend myself to His higher wisdom — . Since God is entirely good, he considered the request. He placed the toady in a place where nothing happened and thus where nothing could happen to the toady, among the judges of the royal imperial ministerium. He carefully removed all of the bones of his body, gave him a skin that was as smooth and leathery as contact paper, and an oil enema for a soul. With the help of this armor, the toady became very pleasant and differentiated himself from a common crawler greatly to his own advantage. One tramples upon a crawler, which takes a bit — if not a great deal — of energy, but if one has toadies, one remains comfortably sitting in one's office chair; & on this occasion — on the occasion of this sitting — the toady pushes itself forward, & usurps the inner world of its superior. One doesn't notice it, but once he has arrived, the toady becomes an indispensable convenience.

The toady is lovable, which is already shown in the diminutive term; a plain toad is something else. He never has his own opinion, but always that of his superiors; & if a toady is really skilled, he has his superior's opinion even before he himself has it. In doubtful cases, he can manage a case so that any opinion can be interpreted from it. For this purpose, he invented the ministerial style, which is something like when one peels an apple in a single long spiral and then places it on the ground; if someone steps on it, he will slip & fall, but the law clerk already stands there and anticipates his superior's opinion, in whatever direction he leans, and expects a decision that accords with the great wisdom of his superior.

A particular strength of the toady is his memory for precedents. Since he himself, as was explained in the introduction, was only created on the basis of God's earlier acts, he admits of nothing in the world that cannot be taken care of with the help of precedents. A toady would never expect an original decision of his boss, and even if it were a matter of creating the world anew, he would know that it had already existed once in the way that Mr. Ministerial Counsel X had made it, and also how it would be received. For this reason also, the toady has an especially good memory for all personnel data. If the world despises it.... In cases where there is no precedent, he looks first at what this or that person has said about it here or there.

It goes without saying that the two great achievements that toadies aim for in the ministries have resulted in the fact that they are legion in all the professions. According to a statement that Representative L. made upon greeting Representative Wense, — although this could just be the private opinion of Mr. L. — they might even become department heads. Today there are toadies among politicians too, among writers, critics, journalists; yes, there are even toadies of propriety and toadies with devoted convictions. Naturally, they conform in each case to their milieu, and it is very difficult to characterize them in general so that anyone can immediately detect them. One must have a nose for it, for they are like smells whose fundamental characteristic is a lack of substance and the ability to insinuate themselves through every key hole. They have no permanent form and are thus always there when something is happening. They never do evil and never good, but they make sure that dealings between all the evil and all the good in the world remain upright. They consist of nothing at all but personal relationships, without being persons; one can tell by their comings and goings whether all is going well for oneself or whether people talk about one or not, whether one inhabits an important position in the world at the moment and to what extent. For this reason they are indispensable. Even the blessed God himself probably wouldn't know, if he had not created them by mistake, whether he stood in the center of attention or was already *passé*.

THE RACE HORSE OF GENIUS[36]

Meeting of the immortals. After everyone sits down, the entrance to the Academy is closed until further notice.

One sees the brows of thinkers. Faces in which the life of the times throbs.

The President: Immortals! I beg our newest member to excuse us for not rising to greet him. We are proud that we cannot do so. The Academy of Literature, which initially — as we are happy to admit — was received by the public with considerable mistrust, indeed, even with smirks, has achieved recognition. A hearty & persevering spirit such as my own could not have expected anything less. In an age where economics plays such a large role, and amid an idealistic but impoverished people, the connection between economics and the irrepressible requirements of humanism had to be made. The economic advantage that it grants was also the first thing that the public grasped about the nature of the Academy.

We are not clear ourselves which cultural tasks the academy should perform. But we are in agreement that these tasks must exist. Those members who joined us only later have made that quite clear to us. Prior to their admittance, they maintained that the Academy was an utterly useless, antiquated establishment, which fostered personal connections, from which they were unjustly excluded; and the first thing they did after they were accepted was to declare that they could not condone such a criticism, since it is in fact our duty to take advantage of the possibilities offered by the Academy in the service of German culture. We do not, thus, want to underestimate the economic advantages; the ideas will come after, and we all hope that something or other will occur to us that will be of great help to the literature of Germany.

The crush of applications to the Academy under these circumstances naturally grew very large. We have looked at the artistic merit, at the number of editions, at instances of luck, at personal connections, at national interests, at intrigues — but all of this was not sufficient to limit the elite immortals of German literature within fixed boundaries. It is impossible to say who belongs in the Academy, and even less who would presume to belong. Everyone. Which is why we have temporarily barred further entrance — by remaining firmly in our seats.

Today we induct our last member. After much consideration, we simply could not deny his merits, and I give the floor over now to our immortal friend, the racehorse Blunderbuss, for his acceptance speech.

Blunderbuss: Immortals!

It was probably 25 years ago when a sports journalist dared to write down the phrase: the racehorse of genius.

He was referring to my forefather Ferror. But you are the first to have the courage to bring the contemporary trend to its rightful conclusion, and to admit me into the circle of the crowned minds of the nation. I will attempt to show you my thanks, by elaborating the reason for your forward-looking and yet so timely decision, which has indeed honored me, but moreover the principle that we all serve.

Members of the Academy! What would happen if Plato, from whose Academy ours has inherited its name, were to visit the editorial offices of a newspaper? ... And such a response would be quite in order. That is the importance of popularity. Or, expressed along more academic lines, of the number of editions.

But your conscience tells you that Courths-Mahler[37] runs to more editions, that *The Merry Widow* is performed more often than Madame Lescau,[38] yes, even more often than the contest between the shadow & the silent one. How can you accept this in good conscience?

Immortals, you do not entirely believe in the magic of a commercial success, yet you do believe to a certain extent in this magic. You are convinced that one can be a bad writer and have a high print run, but you are not convinced that one can be a great writer and have a small one. That is not a contradiction, though the relationship is murky. Allow me to hope that my experience as a race horse might perhaps be of assistance. A great race horse is not conceivable without high bets. The interests of breeder, owner, trainer, rider, club, bookie, bettors, announcers, all depend upon him. This is how it is in literature as well. We animals have the proverb: Where pigeons are, pigeons fly. In your words: Where kings build, cart drivers find work. It is the same thing. The man who invests his ten Marks on my victory or on your book will come forth more readily if the bustle around us is impressive. And it is exclusively for this man that we work; that is, so that he invests his money in the best way.

Nevertheless, if we also nurture success in the service of the nation's development with a certain prudence, we must acknowledge that this development does not depend upon success alone. The sports journalists have never, for example, called a fencer or a trotting horse a genius, but, from a deep instinct, only a galloping horse, a boxer, or a soccer ace. It depends here on two things: one has to touch the heart of the people, and one must possess a certain quality of nobility.

Let me speak of the latter first. I am mindful of being in an awkward position, because my words could easily offend you, since a noble race horse can be unanimously admired and recognized to an extent that is not usually granted to yourselves. I must once again speak about success. We do not have admiration to thank for our success, but rather the admiration comes thanks to our success, although in your case this relationship is a result of a certain liberal equipoise and mutual advancement. But let us not allow this distinction to make us forget the idealism of our nation. The nation will admire; yes, it must. It is a nation that has already possessed and admired many great writers. These writers are dead and yet the admiring words are left over. You know, a widow marries much more easily than a virgin — the function of admiration imperiously clamors for a new object. Once again I take my example from the animal world: it happens that in the mating season one finds dead male frogs grasping on to a little piece of wood. The same thing happens to critics, to essayists, to biographers, to social commentators, to admirers of all kinds: they grasp on, in order to be free of their words and sentences, they grasp on to everything, but, at best, onto something that is already solidly fixed. The noble quality consists in arousing noble qualities.

Let me cast a comparative glance at the spiritual qualities of a literary — of a running genius.

"THERE, WHERE YOU ARE NOT"

[*Susanna's Third Letter*][39]

There, where you are not. Motto: — "It calls me back with the spirit's hiss: There where you a-a-a-r-e not, there is bliss" — [40]

My Dear! As much as one would like to, it is impossible to talk to the former Austrian Chancellor and current professor of moral theology Seipel[41] about questions of impropriety, because in the end even here it is ultimately a matter of experience; but one must give him this, that of all the statesmen who make the world unsafe, he is by far the most spiritually trustworthy of them all. Recently, under his patronage, a scholarly committee was founded to investigate our century's disastrous Nationalism craze and to investigate the nation in all its ways and means. Professor Seipel gave a speech about it, which he spoke of as the groundwork, wherein he openly called the nation of today "ripe for destruction." And this is a glowing testimony to Seipel, since no other European statesman has yet had the courage to say this publicly, although it is a thought that has been ripe since the war. Perhaps because, if you will allow me a small bit of frivolity, if you remove the state from *statesman*, there is nothing but *man* left, & with most elderly men this "man" is rather a little thing, especially as they are accustomed to performing the act of state, which, when compared to the act with a common woman, offers the advantageous stimulations of a gigantic lady.

Our friend Horthy[42] for example — whom you also know — the Hungarian Regent[43] was a simple navy officer before the war; before he began to decay.[44] He socialized with us. A very nice fellow. A little limited, you will say, but it seemed very natural in him: look at the way this man speaks now, since he has become an historical figure! I once picked up a proclamation that he issued[45] when he was at the head of the reactionary faction loyal to the king who slew the Hungarian bolshevists & then occupied Budapest in 1919: "We have loved Budapest tenderly. Here on the shores of the Danube I call the Hungarian capital before the chair of judgment. This city has denied its past, its crown, and has trod its national colors into the dust and attired itself in red rags... But the nearer we approached, the more did the ice begin to melt in our hearts, and now we are prepared to forgive. We forgive, if this misled city... loves this clod of earth with its whole heart and with its whole soul again, loves the crown again and the double cross, loves again its three hills & its four rivers, in a word, the Hungarian Fatherland & the Hungarian race." After he spoke in this way, he saw to it that thousands of people would be hung, beaten to death, and annihilated. If this poetry strikes you — as a Berliner — as something south-eastern, do not forget the Germanic poetry and the Great Fritz,[46] the "liberated nations," or the speeches of Mr. Poincaré. Streams of blood and folly have flowed from all of these poetries. And if the people knew how dangerous bad poetry is to them, they would take more care to foster good poetry. For they can't help it, as soon as they have done something that seems uncommon to them, they are utterly prey to the poetic conception with which it is imbued. That is thoroughly & totally a perversion. While they speak, a professor really turns into a Timur.[47] Indeed, the nice brave Horthy becomes a fat squire from the 16th century, who wipes great words from his beard. Like a shepherd who hunts lambs from one side of the fold to the other in an attempt to catch a few.

People are awfully nice when their life is bearing down directly on their shoulders. And are so insufferable as soon as they are a little bit padded. Why is this so? I will show you with one example what I mean: Horthy. Max[imum][48] — Giant ABC. Really, as if they wanted to write it out in capital letters; so clumsy. Look at a treaty: what kind of language, what a masquerade of a language! They can't do great things naturally. I am certain that the phrases of Versailles & Saint Germain are complicit in the injustices and stupidities of these treaties. Just as the rabble-rousing of the newspapers during the war was a result of the horns which they blew into. For: as they talk, they "talk themselves into" — and they are totally prey to a perversion. I would rather reveal to you the secret at the bottom of all this: Mankind is not finished, he is not solid.[49] Be horrified — it is a fact! That from the top to the bottom there is a canal bored through us, alongside of which we have settled like industrial cities along a river, or as irrigated fields in bloom, is a small bit of self-awareness compared to the fact that our soul is a half-fixed porous cloud, that cannot find its peace in any one form, but that needs forms in order to depict anything at all.

Think first of all of our fashions. At one moment hair is pulled back, & the bust pressed flat against the chest; at one moment the hem rises, then it falls; now we are broad on top and narrow on the bottom; now broad on the bottom and narrow up top, etc. If you do not let yourself be blinded by the abundance of singularities, you will find a small number of geometric possibilities, between which we oscillate in the most extreme fashion, without ever really breaking out of the general circle. The same is the case with colors.

Manni lets himself laugh about this, but Manni is an ass and has no idea how much I desire to and despair of pleasing him.

I have always had some resistance to my own stylishness. It is endlessly silly. It is also endlessly offensive to make oneself, despite all the variations, as similar to all other women as possible. (You can assert as much as you want that personal power unfolds from within conformity — see tradition in the visual arts and architecture, I know, I know — imitation is even stronger there than the creation of new models, and the person who models something for you does you a great service.) Nevertheless: what a rare happiness to be different today than you were yesterday; it grins back at you from the mirror. As is well known, we even make nakedness into a costume for special occasions. A woman who, when she is naked, really has nothing on, can be as beautiful as she wants, she won't make a man warm.

For men have, in place of our constant costuming, the history of the world and of art: they act as if they were only keeping up with our fashions to be nice, in a seemingly blasé way. A little tiny step here, a little tiny step there; one can describe their fashion principle as a maximum of variation with a minimum of changes.

I will tell you right away that this is more than a cheap comparison, namely a very precious truth: that man, as cause for that which he is or does, always puts forth something that doesn't exist. I will show this to you with his seemingly most real invention, race.[50] In other contexts: the nation, the state, and similar types of things. It is always something that doesn't exist in reality. I fear it is already a banality today, when I say that the solidarity among the industrialists or among the workers is greater than that of the nation or the state.[51]

Which is no obstacle to the fact that this bogey of nation or of state has an enormous power at certain times.

This is it precisely: reality only produces pleasure when it is supplemented by something that isn't reality.

But it is really very amusing, this epoch or *Zeitgeist*, which our men attribute to specific periods of the past in order to say that we don't have any of our own, or that they don't know what sort we have. They say: the gothic man, the classical man, etc. That is, they place a person as a middle point, as a center of emanation, or the other way around, as a product of mysterious transformations. That is the same as if we women (the example is rather antiquated) wanted to say, Frau A's reputation is the exact reflection of her essence or the product of the mysterious circumstances of the times. In reality it is the success of certain things that she does, without knowing too much about why, and of the gossip that we spread about these things.[52] History is created in just this way — from the periphery, from accidents, admixtures, etc. ... That is important, because our men think that it is one of their most important duties to make history, and to make it retroactively. Always after the fact. The facts are the things that create *fait accompli*, that throw the whole thing over the heap. This would be very pretty if the people of action weren't lummoxes themselves, like Mussolini.

But all of this has no other goal than to replace that which is with that which is not. Because what exists has a hole in it. God knows where the men get this illogical need; but they do have it; and every metaphor shows this already. Man is a plastic mass. And sometimes is astonished by this.

4.

UNPUBLISHED GLOSSES

EMOTIONAL ILLUSIONS

As a young man, perhaps in one's first years as a university student, one follows a woman in a picture gallery... This meadow-svelte, springtime-meagerness and springtime-nakedness of the spirit, these boyhood longings, when the world, which today is all enclosed, is a spiritual palestra. Nothing unfinished, but rather a type. As a man, later, one loves in the second year, & suddenly thinks: what was it like in those days, at first? Yes, was it... Something stood open. What is that?

It is an emotional phenomenon, the only angle from which it is worthwhile to talk about ideals.

There is something ineffable in the vision of the future; things have a fourth dimension... There is something mild in looking backwards, like looking backward at a garden in autumn.

And the perspectival law makes itself felt, that things assemble into close clusters, & form itself has an aroma.

But sometimes one has the disconcerting experience that behind one's beloved whom one possesses, a second one rises up, to whom one has never spoken. It is the woman with the red hair, etc.

Perhaps God is like this. I have never experienced him. But perhaps the little Joan of Arc from Domremy saw him like that. Perhaps Pastor Schleiermacher, in rare moments, which allowed him to describe him.... Perhaps one should only call things that one experiences like this ideals. *Visio beata* ... ἄπλωσίς.[53]

Now the doctors call it hysteria, delusions, and the like. The connection should not be contested. But where is there not a connection between the pathological and the psychological? The dream, the child's lie, the erotic bite, tiredness — on the other hand, the so-called perversities are normal in the animal world. There are probably no differences in actuality, only in the assessment. In any case, we have no cause to speak of the phenomenon as such as pathological. It depends on its place in the individual and in the life of the individual. (How clearly one thinks about such things these days.)

And here we have the question of how one should place one's self *vis à vis* one's ideals.

The saint was a milkmaid in men's hose; the penitent had lice as a result of his asceticism; the hero is penned in like an animal by his action, by the experience of his heroism. His clothes are drenched with blood, sweat, and dust; they are like boards; he can't bathe; they chafe him until he is sore; they hang stiffly from him as he rattles like a mad kernel inside his shell. His field of vision is reduced to the *forca centralis*; his sight nails itself firmly to the objects. Every violent achievement has something pathological about it, a limited awareness, a last, progressive, swirling ascent. The unhappy Göben.[54] The ideal is always rather doubtful while one is alive. Only afterwards, through deformation... etc.

The ideal of the ideal is a pathological condition. The monotone. It is something that contradicts the typology of mankind, which contradicts the requirements of the primary characteristics of consciousness. It cannot be achieved by us; the ideal is itself an ideal (at its height a Tirolean farmer, an American cowherd, and the like). Those ideals that are tempered by reason are surrogates; they are narcotics. The hero, the saint, the man of reason, will not be tricked; they need an adhesive to hold their lives together. In reality ideals are limits, thresholds, a collection of curves in the imaginary realm surrounding our real life.

Whatever will become real must have a median weight. Life only follows a median line. But whatever remains after this conforming, since it is from the start something which does not fit into real life, creates — perhaps spurred on by certain dissatisfactions & deviations from real life — like the formation of hysterical-traumatic imaginings — the world of ideals. Life does not strive toward the world of ideals, but attracts it toward itself, in the way a street attracts certain foliage.

[...]

As a boy in the first years at university: a meadow-svelte, springtime-meagerness, and springtime nakedness of the spirit, which never recurs. Women know how to treasure it erotically, when the world wraps itself like a spiritual palestra around the narrow soul, which is still wholly tooth and hunger and raw bitter need, certainly also something unfinished. But to their disadvantage, men do not understand this *intermundium* of spirit, filled with attractions that will come only once; and whoever wants to measure the hate that separates the *Reich* of ideals of which I speak from the German *Reich*, or from any other similar kind of human construct, should just consider the word boy in the context of his fellow students and university professors... One wanders as a boy sometimes — once behind a woman in a picture gallery. One sees the pictures she stands before. And feels suddenly: You are the one. You! The woman goes away. One watches a car drive off. The pictures have no more genius. One didn't know the woman. It was something for which there are no words, only likenesses from the realm of bodily sensations will do, out of dreams, from wind, from water, from undulations over fields, under the overall fallen breadth of the evening.

BUDAPEST

At eight o'clock in the morning in front of the windows, if one throws open the heavy wooden shutters — before then I don't know — air that shines white as chalk. A summer's day in Budapest. Hastily jolting cars on hard pavement, in between light cloppings and rubber wheels, in between the roaring motorcycles of the mailmen, who open the mailboxes, screams, cries — a fierce, hardy, business-bustling life — Herr Salomon Wirz & Herr Roszenthal don't have any time, but Herr István Donothing and Herr Jószef Havenothing do have time, and recline on a doormat on the shadow-warm stones, and the servant sleeps on the curbstone, and the women stand around & laugh, and everyone eyes every other passerby. A dollar life, and to boot, the time to enjoy air, light, woman, man, a good horse harness, & everything that catches one's eye. Men sit with fans in the coffee houses. Women walk around on the street in their bathrobes. Scarves in colors so bright that not even the Parisian painters could conceive it. Fine shoes, those of the elegants, perhaps only slightly less beautiful, or perhaps just as beautiful as in London or in Vienna; those of the lower classes inexplicably reminiscent of Italy. Many bare feet.

With or without slippers. Farmer women sit with their legs spread wide apart and offer fruit for sale. Every man sees every woman, every woman every man. Thousands of possibilities. Never rudeness. The workers — in contrast to those in Austria — just as cocky as in Berlin, but chivalrous; one is not molested. The well-known national pride, many monuments to people who do not interest us. Better than the ones in Berlin, but still bad. One eats well in cheap taverns. A wonderful park on Margaret Island. Something in the air, in the imponderables — the way a tree is placed here, the way one sees a shrub there — makes it far better than the Tiergarten, "which cannot be beat." If one reads the store signs: Weisz, Rosenbaum, Perles, Frankfurter — almost every other one German — every superior person speaks German — genuine Viennese carriage drivers & waiters — German blood in one or another mixture — that is what is peculiar, instructive. I can't express in percentages how much Magyar nobility and peasantry, how much Viennese-tinged Austrian export, has its effect here. In any case, one feels the German-Austrian elements clearly and is astounded by an accentuation, an increased strain of Germanness — astounded by possibilities! Travel to Budapest & become Berliners again, but Berliners who visited Budapest.

But please, why should one write travel reports for the newspaper? Objectivity? Chutzpah, as one says in the West of Berlin? Subjectivity! Yes, but the moral element? Some kind of enrichment of life. Expansion (alongside the socio-political goal of earning money). A concierge at the Comitatus Hall: in the space between collarbone & hips. 55 buttons & 44 braids, and jackboots with spurs.

Slice of life. Scoops of Kugler ice cream.

Budapest

Fischer, Adler, Weinmann, Deutsch, Eckbauer, Kransz — Friedmann, Schmitt, Neumann, Politzer, Neidenbach, János, Jakob, Miklos, Antal, Jozsef....

LITTLE (BAD) MOOD PICTURE[55]

Why should a journalist be upstanding? Is that his function? He should think. Then he will be honored and feared. But is thinking something honorable? In its intuitive part certainly not. The journalist is not the leveling factor; the publisher is. Otherwise, there is no way out of the unholy transmutation of roles wherein a Eucken[56] gives the modern soul emotional content and a Kerr is supposed to be proper. But to mistake these two...

I am not speaking of those who are not really journalists. They will have to be chained up; and as far as I am concerned, if one can't catch them by their stupidity, then let us catch them by their morality. But, with respect to a few of them, one might at least exact a passive decorum.

I would like to speak about a new type of journalist, one that I do not yet know to exist.

One only finds form when one has content. What foolishness to demand form from journalists, when one takes content away from them. The shabbily printed repetition of personal anecdotes as in German-American newspapers. The well-known solid ambition of the magistrate's sort.

With Harden,[57] who amuses himself by taming lifeless snake sentences, we have engaged in an investigation of a word of honor. At the time, there was a lively discussion of the extremely tragic case of Göben,[58] asking whether the German press should ban such filth from its columns or not.

Little (Bad) Mood Picture

Peace has been restored. Clarity is what is gained from the German tendency toward moral correctness. Even if one looks back as far as ten years, after every scandal German public opinion proffers an image of a freshly scrubbed room. The floor is mopped, the little windows shine, & the little placemats that just moments before were in tatters lie ironed and bleached in their places. A modest artistic urge hops, feathered, within the little farmer at his window, and whistles so beautifully. Healthy, simple, familiar thoughts reign in clarity — intellectual events do not take place in such spaces. The behavior of caretakers, who sometimes dine with their feudal masters.

But before a scandal, journalism always presents an image of emphatically upstanding, but errant people. The gallivanting of mimes in little city theaters, as they are gradually raised to the status of honored citizens. As if the wife of Wotan were to stride through the Wagner Association gala in a black silk dress, or our colleague

Johannes Vockeraths[59] were to arrange an affair of honor with an officer whom he met one night in a wine bar. One might imagine that the long cowering, disrespectful, badly-formed internal uncertainty of the profession would suddenly burst out again in zealousness. The secret sympathies of the writers are always on the side of the public trade functionary, as soon as he is personally, not only objectively, attacked; even where these two things cannot be separated. Even in liberal newspapers we find this sympathy, which is really a form of servility. It ought to be handled properly. But without further ado one accepts a code of conduct established by the functionary's own circle; isn't such usage subordination? And we must not forget that at the time of the extremely tragic case of Göben (which was more than a personal matter) many members of the press discussed whether they should ban such filth from their columns or not. They immediately fear that the whole profession could lose the indulgence it enjoys. And the phrase passive resistance appears.

What is passive resistance? Something that was of the moment a few times. We remember. The civil servants' strike enacted by precisely following the rules. It was invented in other countries; foolish nations far from Prussia. Perhaps — one asks oneself between one's four clean walls — it is an uncommon corruption, perhaps an uncommon misery. What does it matter to us? The portrait of Kant hangs in despair over German morality like lithographs of rulers on the bare walls of barracks rooms, and the only thing European about this is the immorality, which consists just as much in precise obedience as in individual opposition.

Morality — generalized — is a gigantic slingshot. Perhaps one must not only represent the rights of above-average people, but also the right to disturb the peace. Out of a religious respect for inconsistency. An extreme respect for the last individual phenomenon of intellectual honesty. There are no norms. Only guidelines.

What is proper in Kerr's stories in one context is improper in another's.

Little (Bad) Mood Picture

Peace: clarity is what is gained from the German tendency toward moral correctness. Even if one looks back as far as ten years, after every scandal German public opinion proffers an image of a freshly scrubbed room. The floor is mopped, the little windows shine, and the little placemats that just moments before were in tatters lie ironed and bleached in their places. A modest artistic urge hops, feathered, within the little farmer at his window, and whistles so beautifully. Little theologians bloom. Healthy, simple, familiar thoughts reign in clarity — intellectual events do not take place in such spaces.

Scandal. It is so paralyzing, one knows — these people who build wonderful precision machines, sleep with the field officers' rule book, organize global business, one knows — these people will be there again on the next occasion that calls for mental exertion....

Storm: but at such times, insofar as one reads newspapers (or listens to speeches by cultural leaders), one hears of the experience of emphatically upstanding but errant people, something like: the gallivanting of mimes in small city theaters, when they gradually become... "ours" (attaining a reputation). It is as if the wife of Wotan were to stride through the Wagner Association gala in a black silk dress or our colleague Johannes Vockeraths were to arrange an affair of honor with an officer whom he met one night in a wine bar.[60] The unrelenting attachment of people who have no individual essence to the external implications of ceremonial acts. The longing of bourgeois people for romanticism is strange, but that of truly romantic people for correctness is even stranger. The most valued possession of the Germans is a clean white vest.[61] Not as if things never happen on the sly....

There are two kinds of ideals. Those that one — rightfully — never sees as clearly individuated, like a mountain path where one just grips the next hold & only has the drive to climb upward — and those that are really the remains of decay, of detritus. These are not goals, but consequences, in the way that streets attract certain flora to them, like mist over water. Many official ideals are of this sort. (As clinically assessed, relatively valuable constructions, they would be good just because they represent opposition.) As soon as they are worshiped they become carrion. The artists feel compelled to insult them. Their defense falls to public opinion. Only the public's opinion is "championed." It is sad to think of the journalist as he might be. These are people who have nothing to do with the morality they express. The morality with which they deal is a professional morality. The duty of the profession should be to think more vitally, to sense and to feel more agilely. Swift swimmers in a stream of events. Inventors of new movements, spiritual capabilities; imitators, seekers, experimenters — everything does not always have to be in itself valuable — or at least reasonable people, who let others advise them, and who have the sense to keep quiet when they don't understand something (ready to glean the new tendencies of morality from each new event). But instead, journalists prefer to be defenders of laws (minutiæ in attrition). Country parsons. Incapable of laughing with an anarchist or even of learning from him, associating with him. Incapable even of the intellectual liberality of a professor, who can understand and explain something, without endorsing it. Even if they can't all be producers, does this mean they all have to be bad observers too? Perverted observers. They mistake... the value of the organ of... life, which is spirit, with another organ — the one they sit on. This is the cause. On the Germans... Act as if [what is true for you is true for all men].[62]

This indeterminate saying — not without greatness — is like a cankered growth...

Jotting

Duncan with her theological legs. Wildenbruch.[63] He fills old armor with resounding speeches. Folk art: if I wanted to orient myself about Klimt I would not ask Herr Umlicke from Little Hamburger Street. I'd be even less likely to ask Herr Schoolmaster Bahn [from] Groß Lichterfelde or Friedenau.

This is how clever — or, rather, how flexible — the nation is in matters of research. Not unmitigatedly reasonable, but nevertheless remarkably tolerant in response to visual art; it allows the depiction of nakedness. And, protected by its God-Bless-Art stance against any accusation of sanctimoniousness, it boosts thus the import of whatever else it does.

German state functionaries are certainly virtuous, but since 1870 they are also committed to Blood and Iron, and to the demand for a hurrah-propagation-sensuality to the tune of at least four children.

THE RED HAT

A red hat amid blue & brown hats, amid top hats & bare heads and amid the pale, already somewhat darkened, somewhat benumbed and more stuttering veterans of the battle of light taking place upon the walls. A red hat, the way water in a fountain is always thrust to the top and still always comes back down. A victor in the battle of Manet's cool unsaturated spectrum, like a sudden red lantern swinging in an undifferentiated grey. Manet's people watch from the wall. They have a strain of a painful "we can no longer make ourselves clearly understood" on their lips, in their limbs. And above all — red hat blowing like a cherry tree with glistening fruit — is it not altogether strange when people, one next to the other, look out from flat walls? Or don't you feel that way too? The three-dimensionality — a fiction that manages to be maintained within the picture — is practically compressed to two dimensions by the surrounding pictures. Thus sometimes people like us appear, and then, strangely, there are creatures living in flatness. If in a puppet show someone suddenly takes his head off and carries it under his arm, it is not particularly strange, but if he resembles your female cousin in every feature of his face & in his movements, or if he resembles you yourself, how would you feel?

If something totally senseless, dreamily distorted and distended steps right up to you and introduces itself with an innocent smile, so that you can think of no defense? Perhaps someday someone else will paint painting. The similarity of people to pictures. The fantastical lifelessness in people.[64]

Experience it like something that hurts, something one takes one's revenge upon. The three-dimensionality — a fiction that manages to be maintained within the picture — is practically compressed to two dimensions by the surrounding pictures. Strange how we.... Cult of cannibals. (Creatures living in flatness.) And as a product of this furious mad activity, with a tormented furrow between the brows. Something intensified, falsified, falsified beyond mankind. Woman of the red hat: ribbon in hair, gloss on dress, et cetera, like something falling through the trees, ringing at one moment, the next a thud — slight, but fragrant, aromatic and various, like a soil bed, broken up but made of a thousand creeping, living moments, trickling like warm sand. Poor unsaturated Manet. A red hat....

The Picture Destroyer

The Red Hat

A red hat amid blue and brown hats amid top hats and bare heads & between the bright... pictures of Manet.

A red hat like the way the water of a fountain is always thrust in the air and then always comes back down. Finally, in the battle of Manet's pale unsaturated light spectrum — like a red lantern it swings victoriously in the undifferentiated grey. Manet's people watch from the walls. Strange, when people, one after another, look out from the walls. Red hat — blowing like a cherry tree with glistening fruit — don't you find it barbaric? They have a strain of a painful "we can no longer make ourselves clearly understood" on their lips, in their limbs…

GESSLER GARMENTS[65]

Schoolmasters must have difficulty explaining the injury to honor — obscured by the poetic chronicler's lack of understanding — inherent in the actions of the folk hero William Tell. One may credit him with the fact that his actions were directed against a foreign rule. But in so far as he deliberately refused, against common mores, duty, and usage, to bare his head before the [bailiff Gessler's] hat, he committed an act of conscious contempt. (Compare Count Yorck of Wartenburg's commentary on Schiller's Tell.)[66]

German Social Democracy did not lift its bottom from its seat when the flag at the presidential ceremony was raised for three cheers for the Kaiser. The difference is that it was not a matter of honoring a Gessler, but rather a matter of honoring someone who was in every respect (insofar as that is at all possible) a legitimate ruler. The similarity of the two events begins with the fact that honoring a person who is not even there through rising from one's seat, as is customary, is an abnormally potent sign of submissiveness and respect, which, if only because of the intensity of the emotional expression, is not to the taste of some people.

One can be monarchically minded and still not want to greet the monarch when one meets him on the street. One would be just as unlikely to personally greet a poet or a philosopher whose works one is personally ten-times more thankful for and whom one loves fervently. It is said that the respect does not obtain to the person, but to the principle: but shall we honor principles in a Protestant country in this crudely personalized fetishistic fashion, which is no better than the conception that reformed worshipers have of the holy cult of Catholics?

The entire question is quite similar to the question surrounding the notorious legal situation in Catholic countries whereby a person offends against the (religious) feelings of his fellow citizens by not practicing that religion because he does not have any of these feelings himself. Even if an absence of feelings were to be placed on the same level with an expression of opposing feelings, at least it would still be a question of something unaffected by politics, & among Germans, who keep to themselves, it would be inviolable.

But systematically we see that it is precisely this area that is chosen for the field of operations. — Gymnast, opera house, captain, people's theater, hiker, boy scout... Wrangling for political validation in areas where politicians and functionaries are much too coarse. Unbearable foolishnesses, etc. (Corrupt bestowal of honors these days. In general complete state of deprivation. In the case of the elderly, or the poet, et cetera: Instead, agglomeration in specific places, for example, the monarch.)

PHILOSOPHY OF A SHOE FACTORY

I have the propaganda insert of a daily paper to thank for the suggestions I share here; it was as thick and large as a folio and concerned itself with nothing but the development of the technology, the organization, the charity services, and the economic, political, and moral foundations of a shoe factory. It is the largest shoe factory in the world. It fabricates — . It serves — needs of the world. It employs — workers. It nourishes — people. It is no small thing. Some people would say that such reading is more valuable than a novel. I can't quite contradict them. But since I love novels, I would first like to look at the shoe factory from a literary stand point.

We Standardize

For older readers, who grew up before we were standardized, an explanation is required: in industrial terms, standardization means that everything that can be made uniformly just as well as it can be made differently is made in the same unified way by all factories. That has great advantages, clears away a completely pointless disorder, cheapens and makes life a pleasure. If one wants to change the ink ribbon of a typewriter, one no longer has to search for a brand of typewriter equipment, for all typewriters will have ribbons of the same width and length; and if one loses the rubber on a pedal of one's bicycle, one will no longer find 400 different kinds of pedal rubber advertised at the bicycle shop, among which precisely the one you want is missing, the one that you have in an isolated exemplar on the second pedal. A great number of things are already being standardized — screws, fittings, apertures, armatures, construction parts for pipelines, hospital supplies and laboratory apparatus, tools, luggage — and a great deal more. There are corporations bearing noble names like Fanok and Dechema,[67] and we stand at the beginning of a great spiritual movement, which the Renaissance cannot rival.

It should thus be permissible to make a few preliminary predictions about a time when the standardization movement will refer not only to products, but to people, too. There can be no question that the standardized person will have many advantages when compared to the unstandardized; but despite the fact that great attempts to attain this goal are being undertaken, needless obstacles still stand in its path. Let us start by asking ourselves: what will the standardized person look like? He will be interchangeable. Since today all beautiful people are thin here, but fat in the orient, the accommodation of nature to the average diameter can be assured. The same thing can be said of the standardization of specific degrees of height, which the ready-to-wear industry will require of parents; the Japanese already breed large oily wrestling types alongside the dry-squat jujitsu types by means of special diets. Man will change through his clothes every quarter of a year, but will always look the same; that has almost already been attained today. The need for luxury can easily be stereotyped by proscribed levels of workmanship, just like the tax rate; & in a very refined society one's rank can be symbolized (satisfactorily) by a price tag that reveals that one paid three times as much for one's suit, even though it is the same suit.

These are simple problems. But are not the good person, the moral, the normal, the useful person, aren't the ideal patriot, the ideal disciplined party member, the perfect citizen, already standardized people? Visions of the future are herewith opened up for all standardizing institutions. Just what they have always done, they will now do with the aid and the unquestioned authority of science and technology. The current of the times is moving in a direction that serves their purposes; the last vestiges of the individual are polished away. Love, this ancient forest of eccentricity, will become an utter embarrassment. Who today can still say "you, only you," with a good conscience? Everyone knows that the correct formulation is "you, you typical one."

MONOLOGUE OF A CULTURAL ARISTOCRAT

There is no statement that sounds more reasonable than that we — the rest of us, the people — should be ruled by the intellectually best; that is as evident as it is that the fattest people must eat the largest portions. Cultural aristocracy has the further advantage over the old aristocracy in that one can confer it upon one's self. It is therefore no wonder that so many people today are against the corrosive and levelling effects of socialism, & wish to have an intellectual aristocracy in power — for that is the term that it has become customary to use. The case is best argued for by the fact that even those fat citizens who have always regarded the world as a regulars' round table feel compelled by today's conditions to affirm this.

I too am one of these cultural aristocrats.

Fierce opponents will of course maintain that the really great spirits, if they followed our line and were forced to take over the management of the "people," would have as little of an idea how to rule as they would of how to make a broom or a sailing knot, because their interests lie in a totally different area than the political.[68]

But this statement is based on a great misunderstanding. One has only to consider the situation correctly. How, for example, would the intellectually superior person be recognized? Well, naturally, one would give exams. Masters, Doctorate, Teaching Certificate, and the like. Whoever passes these exams would not have to work in the factory, but would land a correspondingly pleasant position, from which he would automatically proceed to advance little by little over the years. A high school diploma leads to a legal counselor, a doctorate to a minister, if something does not interrupt the process. And only think: would it be much different than it is now? Of course one would have to fulfill special prerequisites to acquire the most advanced managerial positions, or for speedy advancements. But even that is not a difficulty. One must merely ask oneself: how does one become a university professor these days?[69] One must have some ability and have achieved something; but that is not the hardest part at all, since there are always three scholars recommended for every free position, from which one can see that the qualifications for becoming a professor are three times cheaper than the professorship is for the qualifications. The decisive factor is thus first of all that one has better connections. That is how one becomes a high-ranking cultural aristocrat. Even in the bureaucracy, one advances when it is said that one is a clever man, which is difficult to assess in bureaucratic service. Now why not maintain the same selection process in our future society? It is no different today with the great spirits of literature. He who writes cabbage that everyone devours finds many readers, and whoever has many readers is a great man; for whoever earns well helps others to earn, who praise and admire him. Thus, today, we already have a so-called general franchise of authorities and a practically Hungarian voting fraud in this arena.

Perhaps in the future, in cases of socially-confirmed nobility, we will be able to regulate this somewhat better with the help of money, as was the case in the days of royalty; but in general, this vision of the future is really no different from the condition in which we have already placed the intellectual today. The allegation that this is utopian is, as I have shown, thus fully unjustified. At the moment, the only thing that I do not understand is why the current situation seems unjust to me. Perhaps I have allowed myself to be carried away into defending an injustice in a manner unbefitting for a cultural aristocrat.

THE AGE OF THE AUTHORS

(The Golden Age.) There is a legend that there was once an age of the arts. Or is that only a painting from the time of Mackart? Maybe some other people can remember it better: I can only see a naked person blowing into a conch shell — a string strung between two oxen horns, that is the lyre; lions and panthers walk over the grass and are careful not to trample one of the giant flowers that gaze up at the people there; the general impression is of something decidedly before the age of textiles.

Wonderful irony that we have come to call the longing for a gold-less age the golden age. Probably in prehistoric times the king, when the fest was in full swing, presented the singer — who, just like our writers today, went on reading tours — with a golden goblet or a clasp from his robe, and the singer thanked him by inventing the pre-prehistoric age, when all kings and gods were singers themselves. For, when one imagines the golden age of art in detail, one comes to the conclusion that all people & animals in those days must have had money. They carry themselves with an unspoken sense of unconcern about nourishment or acquisition; they doubtless possess everything that they wish for, and have no other task besides expressing their lovely satisfaction in artistic creations. The golden age was an age of amateurs without professionals; if the poet had insisted that he were master of the world — even if it was only a legendary, ancient world — they would have given him poison to drink. He would only have himself to depend on, if he were to utter his pipe dream. And if today, a few thousand years later, a few writers in our bourgeois age wanted to make up a balance sheet, it would turn out that they still believe in the possibility of a golden age, and of exactly the same sort, wherein the owners become poets but the poets never become owners. As they reduce the legendary to the possible, they call it culture or nation or humanity. According to them, the textile industry dealer shouldn't only make worsted yarn, but should also be an enthusiast, a supporter, and a student of the arts.

ON THE NAMES OF SOVEREIGNS & STREETS

It has certainly already occurred to some people that the sovereigns were designated with numbers only as world history approached the present. They were the First or the Second during their lives, & remained thus after their death, or received the supplementary "the Great" (which is also numerical) without other alterations. Admittedly they used Roman numerals, which always look somewhat mysterious. Nevertheless, not even a young man today would be pleased with this, and his mistrust would be immediately awakened if his girl, be it in Roman or Arabic numbers, whispered to him, "You are Erich the Fourth!" But when it came to the love of the people for their sovereigns, we can speak of an Erich the Fortieth.

That such numbering expresses things that should not be actually speaks greatly in its favor. For when the monarchy was still an establishment close to the hearts of the people, the kings, as one still vaguely remembers from one's schooldays, were really called something else; in those days they were called the Bald or the Lame, the Short or the Fat; and if they were called the Great occasionally, it was meant just as honestly as Short-necked or Red-haired: this is reminiscent in the best sense of the names given in criminal circles, such as Sly Max & Crooked Heinrich, or in the suspenseful Indian tales, which should be judged totally without condescension: men who are truly interested in the character of their contemporaries hold on to their flavorful names. And it is clear from this that they were not invented by professors.

Something similar has, as we know, happened with street names. We still keep strictly to the custom of naming them either after some thoroughly unforgettable municipal councilor, or after all of the sovereigns, saints, battles, & philosophers, whose categorization in history makes up just as much of a jumble as the streets themselves. But the difficulties for contemporary people with such faulty memories have already grown so great that in many cities they have begun to allocate sovereigns of literature to the streets of one quarter, all nicely lined up together, & in the neighboring quarter, companionably, the musical geniuses or plant names. Zoology is remarkably neglected here, and with its deep connection to the life of man, serves as a natural reserve for the future; but most of all it is already the case that we don't have much longer to wait before the American custom of designating one street after another simply with numbers is upon us. At best we might save ourselves from this for a time by leaning on chemistry, for in the language system of this complex science every name also contains a hint about the area & neighborhood where one might find the thing designated by it. Without ensuring the chemical correctness of the example, one would live on Ferrocyanurethanbromium Street, & every chauffeur would know immediately where to find it.

Whether this would take hold or not is, of course, questionable.

But it might also be beneficial to ask something else: for why have all the kings been named Franz & Ludwig, Friedrich, Wilhelm, Josef, Georg, Heinrich, Leopold & Humbert and not Emil, Anton, Hans, Paul, Bernhard, Eugen, Wolfgang, Adalbert, and so on? There really seems to have been an arbitrary affront to certain names, and many, from Emil to Adalbert, will gladly say that it serves the sovereigns right if their names no longer suffice and numbers have to be added to them. But the truth is that the royal habit of using only certain names is definitely not a result of an incomprehensible aversion to the others, but of the similarly not quite comprehensible conviction that a ruler, to whom one has given the name of a treasured forefather, becomes a reincarnation of him — so that Otto IV, for example, is not supposed to be merely the fourth, but actually the first Otto returning for the fourth time. It was a magical custom, related to heraldic animals & the like, something that today we would call superstition, if reason were not forced to maintain that only a superstition that still has a recognizable aim can be called a superstition, as, for example, three on a match or knocking on wood.

And we no longer know why we name our own sons & daughters after near relations, even if we vaguely believe that it will bring them some advantage.

In the old days the naming of streets was also different than it is today. Then Budapest Street was really a street that led to Budapest, and not merely something named to honor Budapest, like a sock that one can lay here in one moment and there in another. The blacksmiths worked on Blacksmith Street, the tanners on Tanner Road; if a street was very narrow, it was called the Narrow, and even the houses had their own names. Today that looks like a helplessly disappearing romanticism, which one finds touching in little old cities. One rarely considers that this supposed romanticism would immediately become the most dazzling Berlin novelty if they wanted to name Friedrichstrasse The Grand Stroll, Tauentzienstrasse the Maiden's Walk, and the Kurfürstendamm after one of its functions.[70] Why don't we do this? The truth is that the municipal councilors must fear that they would not be taken seriously if they revealed, while christening a street, that primeval sense of language that melds reality with fantasy. For the contemporary person really has a mysterious dislike of correct language usage; he either takes it for pedantry or a joke. He feels that he is personally exposing himself if he speaks in any way that is other than conventional. He is shy & cowardly with language.

Of Adam it is written: 'And then Adam named with names all the beasts and all the birds of the heavens & all animals on earth.' Today no one but a child does that. Though Lohengrin still sang: "Never shall you ask me [...what my name is]," [71] today only an adulterer or the hero of a detective novel would sing that. But today every virgin can devour a Moor's head or a Lucca eye without anyone thinking badly of them.[72] Thus it seems that it was premature to see in language the distinction between humans and animals, since the progress really proceeds in the opposite direction. It is the case that primitive man was convinced that a person who knew a name also had power over the person or thing bearing that name. Originally, one took language at face value and handled it carefully. Today there is hardly a single person who believes that something would befall him if he were reckless & thoughtless about language. Yet it irritates him that life is becoming more numerical. And herein he is unjust.

FASHION

For the past few years illustrated newspapers have acquired the pretty habit of reproducing fashion pictures from bygone times that a great many of us have lived through, thus going backwards from the years 1914, 1900 to 1870.[73] These series only go back as far as the seventies of the previous century. One sees hats that are like tires or large wheels of cheese, puffy sleeves, fantastical lines from the belly to the throat, and unnatural folds. The first impression is of a comic ineptitude, which our present has escaped rather than emerged from, mixed with the satisfaction of having made so much progress in so few centuries.

But it is not as simple as all that.

First of all: why stop at 1870? A historian of form who is searching for lines of development will easily & naturally trace the line of our clothing back beyond 1870 and into the 1830s, and from there, just as everything follows from something else, into the age of Gœthe, yes, back to the beginnings of bourgeois life. And yet there is a shift in our feelings sometime around 1870, so that everything that is older appears as a historical costume, as if it were in accordance with some requirements of the time; while after 1870 a feeling of pathetic foolishness is aroused in us, just as if we were somehow still responsible for it.

In those days our parents or grandparents were in their best years; in a few more decades, we were. This seems to signify that we are ashamed of that which we don't yet experience as the past or else more or less as the present. For we are ashamed of the ridiculousness of our cast-off clothes.

But why do we put them on?

Ugliness is no obstacle to the rise of a fashion. At first something can be experienced quite clearly as unpleasant, but people give it a try, and after a while it becomes indispensable. The rolled-up trousers that one wears today, for example, were only worn before the war in rainy weather or in the street, & even in Germany they were not considered particularly respectable; today one could, under some circumstances, enter a salon with them on. And women's short skirts, which began to be worn at that time, represent, without question, the most unfavorable phase of womanly appearance conceivable, for they formed a rectangle atop two short little stilts. The fact that these knee-free skirts were practical was no obstacle to their being lengthened since then into impracticalities again, and everything that one wrote and said about the freedom of movement of the new active woman was nothing but the yackety-yack of the times. In truth, utility plays as little a role in fashion as beauty does, and there is no guarantee that we won't be wearing high collars and lace-up boots again.

Naturally, a new fashion always has something appealing about it, but it is probably precisely that quality that will not be understood later on; that is, the condition of being tired of what has come before. A particularity that attracts a generality toward it: a neurotic debilitated way of behaving.

One speaks of the tyranny of fashion and means, among other things, that one has no idea why it changes.

To an extent, one knows that it comes from outside. At most, every two or three years the tailors and milliners must invent something new for business purposes. Sometimes they have more ideas, sometimes fewer; sometimes something nice, sometimes only something absurd. One knows this and feels this & still can't resist the demand that one wear it. This was poignantly obvious in the case of women's short haircuts, a fashion with broader consequences than any other. Only distinctly beautiful in and of itself in a limited number of cases. Poignant year-long hesitation. Deliberation. Probing of the husband & parleying. Deployment of maxims. And finally one tress after another falls under the scissors, so that today it is practically an expression of a determined character, maxims, milieu. If one still....

It is said that one cannot resist the influence of something that everyone does; at first one finds it abstruse and later self-evident. There is something terribly melancholy, humanly poignant, in the fact of fashion. It is the same with other things, but then it is not so directly before our eyes: this is the philosophical significance of fashion.

The fact that one initially sees the new fashions impartially, purely optically, plays a role here. Thus one recognizes them initially as absurd; but later, when one sees them socially, they become symbols of refinement and elegance, according to the richness and taste of their manufacture. Clothes have always been an externalization of social standing. (Endowing the clothes with that which the clothes hide.) To be consistent, one would have to clothe oneself in Dutch guldens or with homely marks. One cause of fashion's inconsistency is its obliqueness. It is well known that it is also erotically oblique. It involves inconsistencies & obliqueness. Consistency and directness would lead to the reform dress.[74]

Today the line of reason seems to lead to nakedness.

But the real truth of fashion consists in this: I can no longer see myself.

THE DOUBLE MAECENAS

Today many people talk and write about whether or not patrons still exist, if they are necessary, and what they do; thus it may be a welcome surprise when one discovers as I did that even *double* patrons still exist. So that we do not give the impression that this story has a moral, let us call them Emporius and Parvenu: their earthly addresses can be made available to inquirers who are serious about indemnity insurance.

They did business in everything that exists, from a silk stocking to the lack of oxygen in the stratosphere, and nobody knew if they were rich. But they owned everything that contributed to an appearance of wealth — palaces, automobiles, pictures, women and horses. It is probably nothing but an empty assertion that to be really wealthy one must have internal riches, and although it may well be that wealth must include something internal, ultimately this is just a fulmination by people who don't possess much more than their virtue. At least that was what Mr. Parvenu thought, who lived the easy life and had pictures of race horses, hunting dogs, and partridges and peaches hanging in his living rooms. But it was not the case with Emporius. He came from a family of secondary school teachers, whom he did not support, but from whom he had inherited something; admittedly it was only the conviction that one must be refined — but it pleased him nevertheless.

Thus his mind was often occupied with how he might support the arts, and he often argued about it with his colleague Parvenu, who irretrievably squandered huge sums on vulgar desires, even though Emporius proved to him that for the same amount of money one could stick pictures on the walls of one's home until it looked like a stamp collection, and that these pictures made just as suitable investments as the stamps. Due to these differences in their cultural stances the two colleagues were mostly at odds with each other, and Emporius decided to show Parvenu once & for all what one had to do if one wanted to attain the position from which one attains still more.

He heard that a famous lyric poet was in the city. He made a visit & invited him to his home. After they had dined like kings, he sat him down, by candlelight under a row of pictures, pulling out a chair from the fifteenth century for himself, and said, "I am a simple salesman, but I know how much is owed to art. Classical pictures do not satisfy me; I want to do something that has never been done before: I am going to fund a great prize for lyric poetry."

The lyric poet opened his eyes wide.

"I will give 3000 marks annually," said Emporius, "for three poems."

In keeping with how lyric poets happen to be, the guest thought that too little.

"It has to be 30,000 marks," conceded Emporius. "Let me think this over. That represents a capital of approximately 400,000 marks; I will give 40,000, so we will have to raise 360,000 more. Listen, we can do that!" They took their coffee in a private office in a thoroughly sober atmosphere; the lyric poet pinched himself in the leg and was assured that it all was real. "We will make Germany the land of poetry," declared Emporius. "Will you work with me? But you alone, Master, despite all the admiration I have for you personally, are not powerful enough. You must gather eleven of the most famous poets as a board of trustees. When that has been done, I will turn to our statesmen and other distinguished personalities, so that they can place their names in the forefront, and when we have come that far, I can guarantee that we will also raise the money. How much, by the way, do you earn monthly with your poems, Master?"

The Master quickly calculated in his head that during the thirty years of his poetic creation he had earned 1,053 marks and 27 pennies. "That is not an impediment," said Emporius. But the Master also told him that he wrote newspaper articles as well, and had a position as reader at a publishing house, which brought in 500 marks a month. Emporius calculated just as quickly: "You will naturally devote almost all of your time to this, and I am happy to pay you half of your income," declared Emporius energetically, "as long as you work with me."

That is how the famous lyric poet earned 250 marks a month out of the cigar budget of his new friend, but the checks were written on the firm's official business ledger, since both of them had agreed to the wish of the poet — who did not want to be less business-like than his partner — to lyrically close on a four-month contract.

At the end of these four months, the eleven great poets had been won over and the well-known lyric poet had been introduced to countless people at the soirées that Emporius hosted. He had paid visits to all of the leaders of politics and finance, the press and high society (the elegant world), and had spread the word that Herr Emporius wanted to herald a new age of poetry in Germany. But when it had advanced to the point when Herr Emporius was supposed to begin his work raising the 360,000 marks, the value of all sorts of expensive merchandise between heaven and silk stockings was suddenly plummeting, and Emporius declared that he himself could not even afford to give his 40,000 — although one really should offer much more to a famous poet — and that maybe the poet should strike out on his own again.

What does a famous lyric poet do on an occasion like this? Well, it depends; there are poets who acquit themselves very well when it comes to the establishment of businesses, but this one gave up and wrote his first poem in a long time. And this story would have ended like this, if the justice of fate had not landed this improvident man in the hospital a year later, placing him in dire need. His friends took up collections for him, since he now only earned his former income of 2.92 marks a month as long as he was able to muster up the mood to write poems, and these friends also turned to Emporius, who had in the meantime achieved a generally recognized position as a patron of the arts. Emporius received them patronizingly, sat them beneath his row of pictures, et cetera, and explained to them that he did not feel obliged to give something for the poet, since he had singlehandedly supported him once already for four months.

However, since the pool of people who have money left over for things that are not precisely their own personal concerns is not great, his friends also went to Parvenu. Parvenu received them in his study, in front of a wall decorated with riding crops and horse shoes, and told them that he also did not feel obliged to do anything for the poet, since even though he thought nothing of poetry, he had already paid for the existence of this poet for four months. When the poet heard this, he became quite healthy from anger — which proves that one should not prematurely judge the benefits of the actions of others — & betook himself to Emporius to have a talk. "What do you want from me?" asked Emporius. "That you renounce your claims," exclaimed the poet recklessly. "If it is nothing more, gladly; you are an oversensitive man!" said Emporius, disapprovingly. The poet betook himself to Parvenu. "In God's name, tell me how you can bring yourself to maintain such lies?!" he asked him — whom he hardly knew — since the two colleagues no longer associated with each other outside of the office. Parvenu politely explained that due to some internal accounting, the checks bore the shared company name. "But what is that to me?!" asked the poet. "True, that is none of your business," conceded Parvenu, "but that is the way it is." "I demand that you renounce such false claims," said the lyric poet. "And you demand nothing more? You are an odd man," replied Parvenu, relieved.

And with that, this story of how someone who had no patrons found two at once must come to an end. Emporius & Parvenu continued to be angry with each other; and since then, if either of them wanted to say something injurious about the other, he would say: "This squanderer once wanted to give up his fortune for the support of poetry!"

GOETHE YEAR

 Gœthe sang:

Through the woods
I went;
Seeking nothing
Was my bent.[76]

In shadows I ſpied
A little flower,
Shining like ſtars,
As little sweet eyes.

I went to pick it,
And finely it said:
Shall I be plucked
To wither dead?

With all its roots
I dug it out,
Brought it to a garden
By a pretty house.

And planted it anew
In a shady bower
Now it grows true
For always & ever.

What experiences Gœthe had! He should be here today! You need only approach the edge of the woods, where the sporting fields are, and suddenly you can hear a gigantic loud speaker. In the middle of the day, when nothing is happening — no world record & no 10,000 meter run — that's what happened to me not long ago. Obviously Gœthe took exercise there. Nowadays one is already accustomed to shop entrances that talk or sentences that fall on one's head when one innocently passes by a radio supply store in the street. But the dimensions make the difference: such a gigantic loud speaker, it boggles the mind; even though we surpassed Gœthe long ago. At first, when the initial sounds come out, it is astounding, as if one were to meet an animal that is much too big. Then one listens — in the air there is a duet of larger-than-life sounds; and when the astonishment & an initial amusement pass, one slowly receives an impression that reminds one of looking at drawings of over-sized heads or nudes: they are so shatteringly great and just a little bit empty. At the same time: their edges have widened, but what is inside them has not. If one wants to draw over-sized heads, one has to equip the eye ultra-microscopically, so that the little bumps and cavities of the skin that were not previously evident become visible and can fill the eye with life. Somehow this applies to the ear as well: the increased amount of volume does not swarm enough with all the sounds that remain unheard — sounds which otherwise would reverberate. Yet if one goes even further, and lets the sounds slowly swell....

END NOTES

1. Birgit Nübel attributes this sentence to Musil's friend, Franz Blei, the editor of *Roland*, where this story was published. Birgit Nübel, "'Die Extraterritorialität der Frau in der Männerwelt': Robert Musils Briefe Susannens," *Musil Forum*, Vol. 33 (2013/14) 177–201.

2. These two letters, published in the illustrated weekly *Roland* in 1925, were to be followed by a third, which remained unfinished, and which is presented in draft form in the "Literary Fragments" section of this volume. See 142–204.

3. The text actually says "may not kill the thief of his honor," which does not seem to make sense in the context of these lines.

4. A parody of Kant's "categorical imperative."

5. From Emerson's essay "Circles."

6. Martha Musil, Robert's wife.

7. A part of Vienna's *Ringstraße*, now called Dr. Karl-Renner Ring, but called the Ring of the 12th of November from 1920 to 1934 to mark the proclamation of the Republic in front of the Parliament building on that date in 1918.

8. Here Musil makes a pun on *Rechtsanwalt* (the word lawyer, which in German contains the word "right"), saying that the *Rechtsanwalt* looked at the *Linksanwalt* (a neologism containing the word "left").

9. Here Musil uses the word "Reflex," which seems to be the wrong word to describe the viewing experience since nothing is visible from the mausoleum referred to herein. Walter Fanta suggests that Musil intends to show the conductor attempting to sound sophisticated by using a foreign word — & using it incorrectly; but Musil may also be suggesting that sensationalistic tourist attractions are intended to create mere thrills or physical jolts.

10. This story appears in Musil's *Nachlaß* in a shorter altered version under the title "The Redeemer" (an early title for the project that became *The Man without Qualities*, c. 1924–25); and prefaced with the subtitle "A Dreadful Chapter: The Dream" (translated by Burton Pike in the *Nachlaß* section of *The Man without Qualities* (New York: Knopf, 1995) 1703–1706). It is followed by the note: "It is probably necessary to say that this is not a true experience but a dream, for no decent person would think such a thing in a waking state" (1706). There are traces in this "dream" of Musil's sex murderer, Moosbrugger, & of Bonadea, the married nymphomaniac.

11. Alfred Kerr (1867–1948), a German theater critic and writer, who wrote an enthusiastic review of Musil's literary premiere, *Young Törleß*, effectively launching his career.

12. The tallest mountain in Switzerland.

13. German, not Austrian, poet & dramatist, 1813–1863.

14. The Komatatschis were bands of Hungarian partisan fighters during the First World War.

15. Reference to the famous Café Gerbeaud of Budapest, founded in 1853 by Henrik Kugler, and known for having the best ice cream in Budapest, as well as delicious cakes & bon-bons.

16. In the Gospel of Luke, two men on their way to Emmaus from Jerusalem meet Jesus, who has freshly arisen from his tomb, but do not recognize him until later that evening.

17. Musil is probably referring to section III.5 of Mill's "On Liberty," which includes this passage: "Yet desires and impulses are as much a part of a perfect human being, as beliefs and restraints: and strong impulses are only perilous when not properly balanced; when one set of aims and inclinations is developed into strength, while others, which ought to co-exist with them, remain weak and inactive. It is not because men's desires are strong that they act ill; it is because their con-

sciences are weak. There is no natural connection between strong impulses and a weak conscience. The natural connection is the other way. To say that one person's desires and feelings are stronger and more various than those of another, is merely to say that he has more of the raw material of human nature, and is therefore capable, perhaps of more evil, but certainly of more good. Strong impulses are but another name for energy. Energy may be turned to bad uses; but more good may always be made of an energetic nature, than of an indolent and impassive one. Those who have most natural feeling, are always those whose cultivated feelings may be made the strongest. The same strong susceptibilities which make the personal impulses vivid and powerful, are also the source from whence are generated the most passionate love of virtue, and the sternest self-control. It is through the cultivation of these, that society both does its duty and protects its interests: not by rejecting the stuff of which heroes are made, because it knows not how to make them." John Stuart Mill, *Utilitarianism, Liberty, and Representative Government* (Maryland: Wildside Press, 2007) 118.

18. Musil is punning here with the German word "Mündigkeit" (majority, maturity), which contains the word "Mund" (mouth), as does the associated term that follows: "Leumund" (reputation).

19. This sentence involves a drawn-out pun including the cognates "währen" (to last) and "Währung" (currency), beginning with the proverb "Ehrlich währt am längsten" (honesty is the best policy, but literally honesty lasts the longest) and continuing with "es währt lang" (it lasts a long time) and concluding with "ist eine umständliche Währung" (is an involved currency).

20. Fencing master.

21. According to Karl Corino, Musil's eminent biographer, Musil based this text upon Leo Frobenius's 1912 book *Und Afrika Sprach: Bericht über den Verlauf der dritten Reise-Periode der D.[eutschen] I.[nner-Afrikanischen] F.[orschungs] E.[xpedition]* (And Africa Spoke: Report on the Progress of the Third Travel Period of the G.[erman] I.[nner] A.[frican] R.[esearch] E.[xpedition]). Translator's personal correspondence with Corino, 2014.

22. Here and elsewhere in this piece, Musil has written ellipses in place of the names of the characters and in one instance for the name of the place where the story occurs. I have substituted them with X's to distinguish these placeholders from other uses of ellipses in this piece.

23. This second passage was written sometime around 1924, while the first cannibal sketch was written

in 1911. We see how Musil continues to keep themes with him and how the note at the end of the previous passage becomes a more fleshed-out scene a decade or so later.

24. Musil has apparently written himself a note here, which I have deleted, reading: "(Novel, lines, supplements II)."

25. Here Musil has tried out the sentence in slightly different syntax: "as into opened boxes into the houses," a construction which, aside from being repetitive, cannot be rendered in English without great awkwardness.

26. Common abbreviated moniker of Peter Altenberg (1859–1919), the notorious Viennese *flâneur* and writer of genre-free small prose that celebrated café society, the demimonde, and beautiful ladies' legs in a light, gay, melancholy style. According to Karl Corino, the dancer described in this piece was Lina Loos (*neé* Carolina Catharina Obertimpfler; 1882–1950). She was an actress under the stage name Lina Vetter and a writer who was married for a short time to the architect Adolf Loos. Peter Altenburg admired her greatly (personal correspondence).

27. Musil's brackets. This is somewhat confusing, as this bracketed section seems to be speaking, suddenly, from the woman's perspective.

28. See *The Man without Qualities*, II, ch. 3: "Start of a New Day in a House of Mourning," where Ulrich, the narrator, remembers his ecstatic childhood experience with animals cut out of a cardboard circus poster: "For at that time the town was placarded with circus posters showing not only horses but lions and tigers, too, and huge splendid dogs that lived on good terms with the splendid beasts. He had stared at these posters a long time before he managed to get one of the richly colored pieces of paper for himself, cut the animals out, and stiffen them with little wooden supports so they could stand up. What happened next can only be compared to drinking that never quenches one's thirst no matter how long one drinks, for there was no end to it, nor, stretching on for weeks, did it get anywhere..." *The Man without Qualities*, Vol. II, tr. by Sophie Wilkins (New York: Knopf, 1995) 749.

29. Here Musil begins a narrative thread with "In Brehm..." but does not follow it.

30. Alfred Kerr, a noted Austrian critic admired by Musil, who launched Musil's career with a favorable review of *Young Törleß*; Oskar Bei, critic and editor of the *Neuer Deutscher Rundschau* between 1895–1922.

31. This note refers presumably, not to the famous Café Landtmann in Vienna, but to a branch on

Vienna's outskirts. Karl Corino, whom I queried about the possible significance of the café, shared this quote from Musil's *Nachlaß* with me: "The famous Café Landtmann is on the Viennese Ringstrasse. But the Viennese will not make an excursion there. So there had to be a branch outside of Vienna. And it exists: the Landtmann's rustic inn in the Crown Prince Garden in Schönbrunn. One can make an excursion there from Vienna...." Schönbrunn is only about a twenty-minute drive from the Ringstrasse. What the "history of the altar door" is remains a mystery.

32. Refers to one of Musil's notebooks, where this entry, a note on Musil's own experiences on the Italian front during World War I, can be found: "War. On a mountain top. Valley peaceful like on a summer tour. Behind the barricade of guards one walks like a tourist. Far off duel of heavy artillery. In intervals of 20, 30 seconds and more; reminiscent of boys who throw stones at each other from great distances. Without counting on success, they always let themselves be incited to let loose one more throw. Grenades slamming in the ravine behind Vezzena; ugly black smoke — as if from a burning house — lasts for minutes. Feeling for the poor garlanded hill country of Lavarone. [...] Far off cannon fire: Hardly able to tell whether a gate

has slammed shut or the boards of a barn floor have been hit. But the faint impression is decidedly more closed, rounder, soft. Indistinguishable as time passes." *Klagenfurter Ausgabe (Klagenfurt Edition): Annotated Digital Edition of the Collected Works, Letters & Literary and Biographical Remains, with Transcriptions and Facsimiles of All Manuscripts*. Eds Walter Fanta, Klaus Amann, and Karl Corino, Robert Musil-Institut (Klagenfurt, Austria: Alpen-Adria Universität, 2009). Hereafter listed as *KA*. *Transkriptionen und Faksimiles. Nachlass Hefte. Heft 1 "klein grau I." Heft I/1.*

33. Friedrich Hradezny. According to Karl Corino, Hradezny was a Major in the Austrian *Landesschützen* regiment in Bozen / Bolzano (Capital city of the province of South Tirol). From the middle of December of that year he was, as *Rayonskommandant*, the superior of Musil (who was the commander of the *Landsturm* infantry company 1/24). Friction between them over small formalities impelled Hradezny to relieve Musil of his position as company commander and to relocate him to Rovereto (*KA Personen Register*).

34. Emil Vidale. Musil's detachment commander from January 1 until February 22, 1916 (*KA Personen Register*).

35. The first draft (above) was written between 1918 and 1926, and the second section (following) was written around 1936.

36. According to the annotations to this piece in the *KA*, "This text can provisionally be dated 1924–26, & is connected with Musil's plan for a satirical novel called 'Die Akademie von Dünkelhausen' (The Academy of Dünkelhausen), about which further notes can be found in Notebook 28 (1928–1929). The text must also be read within the context of the establishment of the Prussian Academy of Art's literary section in March of 1926" (*KA Band 15 Erzählerische Fragmente. Die Zwanzig Werke. Satirisch-utopische Experimentalromane. Textgenese. Das geniale Rennpferd*). Although Thomas Mann nominated Musil for membership in 1931, he was rejected on the grounds that he was "too intelligent to be a creative writer." It is clear that the seeds of such a satire may have been present even before the section's inception and certainly before the society's rejection of Musil in favor of... a race horse of genius. See also ch. 13 ("A Race Horse of Genius Crystallizes the Recognition of Being a Man without Qualities") of *The Man without Qualities*.

37. Hedwig Courths-Mahler, originally Ernestine Friederike Elisabeth Mahler (1867–1950), German

author of more than 200 popular novels. "Musil references her often; her success was a symptom for him of cultural decline" (*KA Personen Register*).

38. I.E., *Manon Lascaut,* Puccini's opera, probably intentionally misnamed here.

39. This is an unfinished, unpublished draft from Musil's notes presumed to be a third letter to the previous two "Susanna Letters" because of the address ("My Dear"), the mention of Susanna's husband Manni, and the female persona of the letter writer. The draft has been dated, based on historical clues, around 1924–25.

40. From "Der Fremdling" (The Stranger), text by Georg Philipp Schmidt von Lübeck and melody by Franz Schubert: "I wander soft, am happy ne'er / And ever asks the sigher: where? / It calls me back with the spirit's hiss: / There where you are not, there is bliss!"

41. Ignaz Seipel (1876–1932) was a theologian, prelate, and twice Austrian Federal Chancellor. He resigned his post on June 1, 1924 after an assassination attempt, but became Chancellor again from 1926–1929. In June 1928, Musil, as part of a delegation representing the Austrian Association for the Protection of German Writers, testified before Seipel to protest the introduction of the Austrian version of the German "trash and smut"

laws. See Klaus Amann, *Robert Musil: Literatur und Politik* (Reinbek: Rowohlt Taschenbuch Verlag, 2007) 90: "The negotiation was conducted between the Federal Chancellor and the doyen of Austrian writers, Arthur Schnitzler. The conversation, which was recorded by the President of the 'General Association,' Ernst Lothar, consisted of a strict examination of the 66-year-old writer by the 52-year-old so-called 'prelate without mercy,' & ended with the conclusion by the man of God [Seipel]: "worlds separate us."

42. Miklós Horthy (1868–1957). Hungarian officer and politician who led troops loyal to the Hungarian crown in 1919.

43. Regent: *Reichsverweser*, a word that suggests the word *Verwesung* (decay), inspiring the pun that follows.

44. Decay = *verweste*.

45. In Musil's notebook 19 he records, under the heading "Mirror of the Times," the invasion of Horthy's counterrevolutionary troops into Hungary on November 16, 1919, & includes the passages from Horthy's speech quoted here, preceded by the critique: "Speeches were given which contained not one single word from our present time." After the excerpt from Horthy's speech, Musil concludes:

"Where is Karl Kraus?" — referring most likely to Kraus's persistent critique of the abuse of language. This is one of the only mentions of Kraus by Musil that suggests something like sympathy with him.

46. Friedrich the Great.

47. Uldjaitu-Timur Khan (1265–1307), emperor of the Mongolian Yuan Dynasty in China, son of Dschingkims & grandchild of Kublai Khan. He reigned from 1294–1307 and is known as a supporter of Confucianism. *KA, Personen-Register.*

48. Probably an abbreviation & shorthand for Musil's preoccupation with the mathematical concept of the maximal possible variation within a minimum of variety, which is repeated further on in the text in a reference to men's fashion.

49. This is clearly a reference to Musil's "theorem of human shapelessness," discussed in his essay "The German as Symptom" and elsewhere.

50. In Musil's essay "The Nation as Ideal & Reality," he maintained that race was just an abstraction, but in a later note, in response to reading *Die Rassenidee in der Geistesgeschichte von Ray bis Caru* (The Racial Idea in Cultural Hstory from Ray to Caru), he reconsidered, noting that his earlier position "that there are only individuals and that races 'are something that have to do with individuals' is not

quite sound." "Types," he concludes, are "also to a certain extent realities and not merely categorical terms" (Notebook 30, June 1934).

51. While this construction seems to leave Musil's meaning somewhat ambiguous, in other discussions of this question in Musil's notes he argues that a German worker has more in common with a French worker than with a German factory owner, i.e., that race is not the single determining factor of association or commonality.

52. Another version of this piece contains the following passage: "On Arn[heim]: Herr Cæsar crossed the Rubicon. We don't know why, we will never know. But from individual clues & comparisons we construct a hypothesis. Instead of using historical facts to build models of reality, and instead of perfecting these models more and more as models for the future, they make the opposite use of them — a retroactive method. They explain the past with crude models and construe the present out of the past. They advance history and politics instead of conduct of life. / Later: Conduct of life and genius /" (*KA. Transkriptionen und Faksimiles. Nachlass Mappen. Mappengruppe VI. Mappe VI/2 "Aufsätze."* VI/2/43 Ü 73 2).

53. Although there is some uncertainty about the proper transcription of this Greek word (the

KA presents it as *απλωσίσ*, which has no apparent meaning), a closer inspection of the original facsimile manuscript supports a reading closer to *ἄπλωσίς*, which means "simplification," as opposed to complexity, which could make sense in this context as a commentary on the single-minded focus of the idealist. Thanks are due to Nathanael Carney and Walter Fanta for these elucidations.

54. Hugo von Göben, the subject of another unfinished, unpublished gloss of Musil's, was allegedly urged on by his lover, the nymphomaniac Herta Antonie Schönebeck, to kill her husband, Major Gustav von Schönebeck (*KA*: *Personen Register*).

55. In these fragments, Musil is reacting to a contemporary scandal involving Alfred Kerr (1867–1948), a German theater critic and writer whom he admired, & Traugott von Jagow, the police chief of Berlin in 1909, who was involved in theater censorship cases. The notes of this draft are taken up again in his essay "Das Unanständige und Kranke in der Kunst" (The Obscene & the Pathological in Art), published in the journal *Pan* (which had earlier been confiscated by von Jagow) in 1911 (see *Precision and Soul: Essays and Addresses*, ed. and tr. by David Luft and Burton Pike (Chicago & London: University of Chicago Press, 1990) 3–8). Apparently, when Carl Sternheim's drama "Die

Hose" (Pants, or Underpants) was under threat of censorship, Max Reinhardt, director of the *Deutsches Theater,* invited von Jagow to a dress rehearsal, planting a beautiful actress (who happened to be the wife of Paul Cassirer, the publisher and coeditor with Alfred Kerr & Wilhelm Herzog of the radical journal *Pan* — and a cousin of Ernst Cassirer) beside him to distract him whenever the language got too racy. Von Jagow passed the play, but also made a pass at the actress, invoking cries of hypocrisy and adulterous intentions by the press. "Over the next weeks Kerr and others published several caustic articles, poems, and cartoons about the affair, castigating von Jagow for cynical moral hypocrisy and abusing his office, & ridiculing the double standards in respectable Wilhelmine society." See Gary D. Stark, *Banned In Berlin: Literary Censorship in Imperial Germany, 1871–1918* (New York: Berghahn Books, 2013) 50.

56. Rudolph Christian Eucken (1846–1926), German spiritualist philosopher. See Musil's comment in his essay, "Anmerkung zu einer Metaphysik" (Commentary on a Metaphysics) on Walter Rathenau's *Zur Mechanik des Geistes* (On the Mechanics of the Spirit): "The notion that good works in this world somehow constitute our existence in the next — this pet idea of contemporary spiritualist

philosophy, which no longer has enough confidence to guarantee personal immortality — has about it something of the child's need to take his toy to bed with him at night & into the dark hole of sleep. When combined with inappropriate didacticism there is something devastatingly comical about it, as in the case of Eucken and sometimes even Bergson" (*Precision and Soul*, 54).

57. Maximilian Harden (1892–1927), publicist, actor, & writer.

58. See note 54, above.

59. Character in Gerhart Hauptmann's play, *Einsame Menschen* (1891; Lonely People).

60. This repetition is Musil trying a new version of the piece. His working method was to write in one sweep and then begin again, often repeating large passages verbatim and then adding small changes.

61. A white vest is proverbial in German for being without guilt.

62. A reference to Kant's categorical imperative. See Susanna's Second Letter, where Musil spells this out, putting it in the mouth of Susanna's husband, "Manni," whose pronouncements represent the fallacy of applying general laws to specific situations.

63. Ernst von Wildenbruch (1845–1909), a German poet and dramatist.

64. See Musil's discussion of the still life in his drafts, "Breaths of a Summer's Day," in the *Nachlaß* to *The Man without Qualities* for similar thoughts on the perverse pleasures of non-resistance, dead objects, and necrophilia. Also my chapter, "Still Lives" in *The World as Metaphor in Robert Musil's 'The Man without Qualities'* (New York: Camden House, 2012).

65. Albrecht (Hermann) Gessler was the bailiff whose authoritarian rule led to William Tell's rebellion and the independence of the Old Swiss Confederacy. Legend has it that Gessler placed his hat upon a pole in the town square & demanded that every citizen bow down before it. When Tell, who was a renowned marksman, refused, he was given the choice of immediate death or of shooting an apple off the head of his own son, which latter deed he successfully accomplished.

66. Count Maximillian Yorck von Wartenburg (1850–1900), German military officer, diplomat, and historian, who wrote an essay on Friedrich Schiller, presumably discussing the play *Wilhelm Tell*.

67. Most likely refers to the Dechema Society for Chemical Engineering and Biotechnology, founded in 1926. Fanok was presumably a similar research institution.

68. In his lecture at the Paris International Congress for the Defence of Culture in 1935, Musil himself was one of the people who raised such an objection, noting that although hygiene effects everyone too, he had not practiced either plumbing or politics, because he had "no more talent as a hygienist than" he did "as an economic leader or geologist" (*Precision and Soul*, 264).

69. In a note titled "Genius and Collectivity" from around 1936, Musil complains about the way one becomes a professor in the Nazi era: "filling the Chair of Anatomy at the University of Vienna with a very young man who has written a work on Alpine phrenology or something like that, and literally nothing else!!" See *KA: Transkriptionen und Faksimiles. Nachlass Hefte. Heft 34. "Schwarzes Heft weich"* 34/37. But he was already aware ten years prior of the relative corruptions of academic & social advancements in the pre-fascist period.

70. I.E., as a well-known assignation area for prostitution, still to this day in fact.

71. In Wagner's *Lohengrin*, the hero sings, "Elsa, if I am to become your husband, / If I am to protect country & people for you, / If nothing is ever to take me from you, / Then you must promise me one thing / Never shall you ask me, / Nor trouble yourself to know, / Whence I journeyed, /

What my name is, or my origin!" In this draft, Musil has only included the phrase, "Never shall you ask me," either assuming his readers' recognition of the passage, or planning to add it later to a revised draft.

72. A *Mohrenkopf* is a chocolate pastry; a *Lucca Auge* is an open-faced sandwich consisting of an oyster, caviar, & tartar sauce, named in honor of Pauline Lucca (1841–1908), a prominent operatic soprano, by a chef at Berlin's Hotel Kempinski in 1842.

73. Musil has really written here, "1914, 1900 to 1890," but below he says that the series goes back as far as 1870.

74. The *Reformkleid* was a style of loosely fitting shapeless dress popular among bohemian women in the mid-nineteenth century as part of a health-conscious movement to liberate women from the ill effects of corsets and other restrictions to movement.

75. This text, satirizing the effects of the world economic crisis on art production, is also related to the financial crisis experienced by Musil's publisher Rowohlt, which induced Musil to try to make money by writing a series of glosses (including this one) for the *Berliner Zeitung* (*KA: Lesetexte Band 15. Fragmente aus dem Nachlass. Nachgelassene Glossen. Unzeitgemässes von 1929–1932.*

Der Doppelmäzen. Übersicht). According to Karl Corino, one of the patrons in this piece is modelled on Richard Weininger, the brother of Otto Weininger, the Austrian author of *Sex and Character*.

76. Musil's draft only includes the first stanza of this poem. He either intended to add the rest later or expected his readership to know the reference.

BIBLIOGRAPHY

All of the translated texts have been taken from *Die Klagenfurter Ausgabe (KA): Annotated Digital Edition of the Collected Works, Letters and Literary and Biographical Remains, with Transcriptions & Facsimiles of All Manuscripts*, eds. Walter Fanta, Klaus Amann, and Karl Corino (Klagenfurt, Austria: Alpen-Adria Universität & Robert Musil-Institut, 2009).

Stories

Susanna's Letter. "Brief Susannens." Original printings: *Roland* (1.15.1925); *Prager Presse* (1.21.1925). Posthumous printings: *Akzente* (1963) 649–653; Robert Musil, *Gesammelte Werke*, ed. by Adolf Frisé (Reinbek bei Hamburg: Rowohlt, 1978) 634–637; *KA: Lesetexte: Kleine Prose.*

Susanna's Second Letter (Our Men). "Zweiter Brief Susannens (Unsere Männer)." Original printing: *Roland* (2.5.1925); *Prager Presse* (2.8.1925). Posthumous printings: *Akzente* (1963) 657–660; Frisé (1978) 638–640; *KA: Lesetexte: Kleine Prosa.*

Page From a Diary. "Tagebuchblatt." Original printings: *Berliner Tageblatt* (8.8.1927); *Der Tag* (12.4.1927); *Prager Presse* (1.8.1928). Posthumous printings: Robert Musil, *Gesammelte Werke*, ed. by Adolf Frisé (Reinbek bei Hamburg: Rowohlt, 1955) 796–799; Frisé (1978) 647–649; *KA: Lesetexte: Kleine Prosa.*

The Fairy Tale of the Tailor. "Das Märchen vom Schneider." Original printings: *Der Tag* (11.21.1923); *Prager Presse* (12.25.1923). Posthumous printings: Frisé (1955) 540–542; Frisé (1978) 627–629; *KA: Lesetexte: Kleine Prosa.*

Robert Musil to an Unknown Little Girl. "Robert Musil an ein unbekanntes Fräulein." Original printing: *Berliner Tageblatt* (12.25.1930). Posthumous printings: *Études Germaniques* (1965) 567–568; Frisé (1978) 650–651; *KA: Lesetexte: Kleine Prosa.*

Across Charlottenburg. "Quer Durch Charlottenburg." Original printing: *Berliner Tageblatt* (3.27.1932). Posthumous printings: *Akzente* (1965); Frisé (1978) 654–657; *KA: Lesetexte: Kleine Prosa.*

The Inn on the Outskirts. "Der Vorstadtgasthof." Original printings: *Vers und Prosa* (3.15.1924); *Prager Presse* (9.12.1926); *Pandora Drucke* (1931). Posthumous Printings: Frisé (1957) 577–580; Frisé (1978) 630–634; *KA: Lesetexte: Kleine Prosa.*

Broken Off Moment. "Ausgebrochener Augenblick." Original printing: *Prager Presse* (8.30.1931). Posthumous printings: *Études Germaniques* (1965) 568–570; Frisé (1978) 651–654; *KA: Lesetexte: Kleine Prosa.*

The Storm Tide on Sylt. "Der Sturmflut auf Sylt." Original printing: *Der Tag* (9.20.1923). Posthumous printings: Frisé (1978) 625–627; *KA: Lesetexte. Kleine Prosa.*

The Thirsty Ones. "Die Durstigen." Original printing: *Berliner Tageblatt* (8.14.1926). Posthumous printings: Marie-Louise Roth, "'Die Durstigen.' Ein Unbekannter Text und Seine Deutung." In: *Robert Musil: Studien zu seinem Werk*, eds. Karl Dinklage, Elisabeth Albertsen, and Karl Corino (Klagenfurt: Robert Musil-Archiv, 1970) 71–81; Frisé (1978) 642–647; *KA: Lesetexte: Kleine Prosa*.

Small Journey Through Life. "Kleine Lebensreise." Original printings: *Vossische Zeitung* (6.27.1925); *Magdeburgische Zeitung* (6.15.1926); *Prager Presse* (8.10.1926). Posthumous printings: Frisé (1957) 539–540; Frisé (1978) 640–642; *KA: Lesetexte, Kleine Prosa*.

Glosses

Generation of Styles and Styles of Generations. "Stilgeneration und Generationsstil." Original printings: *Berliner Börsen-Courier* (6.4.1922); *Der Tag* (2.16.1924). (This text is a later version of a piece entitled "Stilgeneration oder Generationstil" (Generation of Styles or Styles of Generation) from 1921, published in *Prager Presse* on 5.14.1921). Posthumous printings: Frisé (1978) 664–667; *KA: Lesetexte: Kleine Prosa*.

Johann Strauss as a Giant. "Johann Strauss als Riese." Original printing: *Prager Presse* (7.6.1921). Posthumous printings: *Études Germaniques* (1965) 567–568; Frisé (1978) 663–664; *KA: Lesetexte: Kleine Prosa*.

The Criminal Lovers. The Story of Two Unhappy Marriages. "Das verbrecherische Liebespaar. Die Geschichte zweier unglücklicher Ehen." Original printing: *Prager Presse* (3.20.1923). Posthumous printings: Frisé (1978) 669–671; *KA: Lesetexte: Kleine Prosa.*

Moral Institutions. "Sittenämter." Original printings: *Prager Tagblatt* (7.7.1923); *Der Tag* (10.10.1923). Posthumous printings: Frisé (1978) 671–674; *KA: Lesetexte: Kleine Prosa.*

The Twilight of War. "Kriegsdämmerung." Original printing: *Roland* (1.1.1925). Posthumous printings: Jürgen C. Thöming, "Wie erkennt man ein anonym veröffentlichten Musil-Text" (How to recognize an anonymously published Musil text?), *Ètudes Germaniques* (1970) 170–183; Frisé (1978) 674–677; *KA: Lesetexte: Kleine Prosa.*

Civilization. "Zivilisation." Original printing: *Roland* (3.11.1925). Posthumous printings: variant under the title, "An der Spitze der Zivilisation" (At the Height of Civilization), Frisé, *Gesammelte Werke* (Reinbeck bei Hamburg: Rowohlt, 1955) 843–844; Frisé (1978) 677–678; *KA: Lesetexte: Kleine Prosa.*

An Example. "Ein Beispiel." Original printing: *Roland* (3.18.1925). Posthumous printings: Frisé (1978) 678–680; *KA: Lesetexte: Kleine Prosa.*

Intensivism. "Intensismus." Original printings: *Berliner Tageblatt* (1926); *Der Tag* (1927). Posthumous printings: Frisé (1978) 681–683; *KA: Lesetexte: Kleine Prosa.*

Speed is Witchery. "Geschwindigkeit ist eine Hexerei." Original printings: *Vossische Zeitung* (5.28.1927); *Prager Presse* (7.6.1927); *Magdeburgische Zeitung* (7.29.1927); *Der Tag* (9.20.1927); *Vierzehn Federn* (1927). Posthumous printings: Frisé (1957) 542–544; Frisé (1978) 683–685; *KA: Lesetexte: Kleine Prosa.*

When Papa Learned to Play Tennis. "Als Papa Tennis Lernte." Original printing: *Der Querschnitt* (April 1931). Posthumous printings: Frisé (1955) 815–820; Frisé (1978) 685–69; *KA: Lesetexte: Kleine Prosa.*

Talking Steel. "Blech Reden." Original printing: *Prager Presse* (10.11.1931). Posthumous printings: Frisé (1955) 846–848; Frisé (1978) 692–694; *KA: Lesetexte: Kleine Prosa.*

The Art and Morality of the Crawl Stroke. "Die Kunst und Moral des Crawlens." Original printing: *Der Querschnitt* (June 1932). Posthumous printings: Frisé (1955) 821–825; Frisé (1978) 694–698; *KA: Lesetexte: Kleine Prosa.*

Literary Fragments

From the Stylized Century: The Street. (January 1900–September 1900). *"Aus dem stilisirten Jahrhunderts: Die Strasse." KA: Lesetexte. Frühe Tagebuchhefte (1899–1926). I. Brünn / Stuttgart / Berlin (1899–1908). 4. Altes schwarzes Heft* (1900–1904). *Tagebuch und Literarische Projekte.*

Cannibals. "Menschenfresser" (1911–1914). Cannibal and Lung Patient Story. "Menschenfresser und Lungenkrankengeschichte" (middle of 1924). *KA: Band 15. Fragmente aus dem Nachlaß: Erzählerische Fragmente. Anfänge und Notizen.*

Travel Notes. "Reiseblätter" (June–July, 1911). *KA: Band 15. Ibid.*

Letter to an Imaginary Man. "Brief an einen Imaginären" (1911–1913). *KA: Band 15. Ibid.*

P. A. & the Dancer. "P. A. und die Tänzerin" (1911–1913). *KA: Band 15. Ibid.*

Summer in the City. "Sommer in der Stadt" (March/April 1912). *KA: Band 15. Ibid.*

Shadow Play in the Small City. "Schattenspiel in der kleinen Stadt" (1920–1922). *KA: Band 15. Ibid.*

War Diary of a Flea. "Kriegstagebuch eines Flohs" (1918–1937). *KA: Band 15. Fragmente aus dem Nachlaß: Erzählerische Fragmente. Satirisch-utopische Experimentalromane.*

The Toady. "Das Schlieferl" (1921–22). *KA: Band 15. Ibid.*

The Race Horse of Genius. "Das geniale Rennpferd" (1924–1926). *KA: Band 15. Ibid.*

(Susanna's Third Letter) There Where You Are Not. "(Dritter Brief Susannens) Da wo du nicht bist" (draft dated around 1924). *KA: Lesetexte: Nachgelassene Glossen.*

Unpublished Glosses

Emotional Illusions. "Emotionillusionen" (1910). *KA: Lesetexte Band 15. Fragmente aus dem Nachlaß. Nachgelassene Glossen. Ideale von 1905–1914. Emotionillusionen.*

Budapest. "Budapest" (1910). *KA: Lesetexte Band 15. Fragmente aus dem Nachlaß. Nachgelassene Glossen. Ideale von 1905–1914. Budapest.*

Little (Bad) Mood Picture. "Verstimmungsbildchen." *KA: Lesetexte Band 15. Fragmente aus dem Nachlaß. Nachgelassene Glossen. Ideale von 1905–1914. Verstimmungsbildchen.*

The Red Hat. "Der rote Hut" (1911–1912). *KA: Lesetexte Band 15. Fragmente aus dem Nachlaß. Nachgelassene Glossen. Ideale von 1905–1914. Der rote Hut.*

Gessler Garments. "Gesslersche Bekleidungstuck" (1913). *KA: Lesetexte Band 15. Fragmente aus dem Nachlaß. Nachgelassene Glossen. Ideale von 1905–1914. Gesslersche Bekleidungstuck.*

Philosophy of a Shoe Factory / We Standardize. "Philosophie einer Schuhfabrik / Wir Normen" (1922–24). *KA: Lesetexte Band 15. Fragmente aus dem Nachlaß. Nachgelassene Glossen. Der Zug der Zeit von 1918 bis 1930. Philosophie einer Schuhfabrik / Wir Normen.*

Monologue of a Cultural Aristocrat. "Monolog eines Geistesaristokraten." 1924–1926. *KA: Lesetexte Band 15. Fragmente aus dem Nachlaß. Nachgelassene Glossen. Der Zug der Zeit von 1918 bis 1930. Monolog eines Geistesaristokraten.*

The Age of the Writers. "Das Zeitalter der Dichter" (1926–1927). *KA: Lesetexte Band 15. Fragmente aus dem Nachlaß. Nachgelassene Glossen. Der Zug der Zeit von 1918 bis 1930. Das Zeitalter der Dichter.*

On the Names of Sovereigns and Streets. "Über Fürsten- und Straßennamen" (1926–1927). *KA: Lesetexte Band 15. Fragmente aus dem Nachlaß. Nachgelassene Glossen. Der Zug der Zeit von 1918 bis 1930. Über Fürsten- und Straßennamen.*

Fashion. "Mode" (1931). *KA: Lesetexte Band 15. Fragmente aus dem Nachlaß. Nachgelassene Glossen. Unzeitgemässes von 1929–1932. Mode.*

The Double Mæcenas. "Der Doppelmäzen" (1931). *KA: Lesetexte Band 15. Fragmente aus dem Nachlaß. Nachgelassene Glossen. Unzeitgemässes von 1929–1932. Der Doppelmäzen.*

Gœthe Year. "Gœthejahr" (1931). *KA: Lesetexte Band 15. Fragmente aus dem Nachlaß. Nachgelassene Glossen. Unzeitgemässes von 1929–1932. Gœthe Jahr.*

ACKNOWLEDGMENTS

I would not have begun to look at these pieces when I did had it not been for Birgit Nübel, who presented a revelatory paper on the "Susanna Letters" at a conference in Klagenfurt, Austria.[1] I thank her for the inspiration, her illuminating commentaries on the pieces, & the honor of her friendship in the realm of Musil scholarship, which remains, despite the years that have passed since Susanna's complaints to her female correspondent, largely a "world of men." In this man's world I am very grateful for the support of Walter Fanta of the International Robert Musil Society, whose expertise in the genealogy of the texts in the *Klagenfurter Ausgabe* has been indispensable to my work. Karl Corino, Musil's eminent biographer, has been generous with his time and knowledge in helping me to solve some riddles in the text and to provide a number of significant contextual notes. Gunther Martens was kind enough to provide me access to a number of his own papers on Musil, which proved very helpful in understanding the role of small prose for Musil and his contemporaries.

1. Later printed as Birgit Nübel, "'Die Extraterritorialität der Frau in der Männerwelt': Robert Musils Briefe Susannens," *Musil Forum*, Vol. 33 (2013/14) 177–201.

ACKNOWLEDGMENTS

I am grateful for a grant from the Austrian Ministry of Arts, Culture, and Education, which has helped me to complete this translation. And for a grant from the National Endowment for the Arts, which enabled me to work on these translations in peace amid the inspiring hum of the Vermont Studio Center (which I came to call the Temple of Work) for a month in March 2014. And I will never forget the kindness and energy of Rosemarie Carruth, who fetched me in below-zero temperatures from the Studio Center campus & brought me through ice & snow to her fairytale house in the woods, to feed me, regale me with tales of her life in Germany & America, and to sit on her couch with me to work through some difficult translation problems I had brought to her. I thank Mark Mirsky of *Fiction* magazine & Douglas Glover of *Numero Cinq* for publishing early excerpts of these translations. I cannot thank Stephen Callahan enough for encouraging me onward in this project & for reading over the manuscript with a level of precision that would have pleased *Monsieur le Vivisecteur* himself. Burton Pike is, of course, the presiding muse of this translation. I thank him for casting an eye over some of my amateur attempts, for admonishing me to pay attention to Musil's rhythm, for setting such a high standard for my work, and for leaving me what turns out to be a great deal of Musil yet to translate. Rainer J. Hanshe of Contra Mundum, my editor & friend, had the boldness and vision to take on this project and to always maneuver through the inevitable publication challenges with grace, wisdom, and good humor, rescuing me many times from the gaping abyss of impending thought crash.

COLOPHON

THOUGHT FLIGHTS

was typeset in InDesign CC.

The text & page numbers are set in *Adobe Jenson Pro.*
The titles are set in *P22 Arts & Crafts.*

Book design & typesetting: Alessandro Segalini
Cover design: Contra Mundum Press
Image credit: Koloman Moser

THOUGHT FLIGHTS

is published by Contra Mundum Press.
Its printer has received Chain of Custody certification from:
The Forest Stewardship Council,
The Programme for the Endorsement of Forest Certification,
& The Sustainable Forestry Initiative.

Contra Mundum Press New York · London · Melbourne

CONTRA MUNDUM PRESS

Dedicated to the value & the indispensable importance of the individual voice, to works that test the boundaries of thought & experience.

The primary aim of Contra Mundum is to publish translations of writers who in their use of form and style are *à rebours*, or who deviate significantly from more programmatic & spurious forms of experimentation. Such writing attests to the volatile nature of modernism. Our preference is for works that have not yet been translated into English, are out of print, or are poorly translated, for writers whose thinking & æsthetics are in opposition to timely or mainstream currents of thought, value systems, or moralities. We also reprint obscure and out-of-print works we consider significant but which have been forgotten, neglected, or overshadowed.

There are many works of fundamental significance to *Weltliteratur* (*& Weltkultur*) that still remain in relative oblivion, works that alter and disrupt standard circuits of thought — these warrant being encountered by the world at large. It is our aim to render them more visible.

For the complete list of forthcoming publications, please visit our website. To be added to our mailing list, send your name and email address to: info@contramundum.net

Contra Mundum Press
P.O. Box 1326
New York, NY 10276
USA

OTHER CONTRA MUNDUM PRESS TITLES

Gilgamesh
Ghérasim Luca, *Self-Shadowing Prey*
Rainer J. Hanshe, *The Abdication*
Walter Jackson Bate, *Negative Capability*
Miklós Szentkuthy, *Marginalia on Casanova*
Fernando Pessoa, *Philosophical Essays*
Elio Petri, *Writings on Cinema & Life*
Friedrich Nietzsche, *The Greek Music Drama*
Richard Foreman, *Plays with Films*
Louis-Auguste Blanqui, *Eternity by the Stars*
Miklós Szentkuthy, *Towards the One & Only Metaphor*
Josef Winkler, *When the Time Comes*
William Wordsworth, *Fragments*
Josef Winkler, *Natura Morta*
Fernando Pessoa, *The Transformation Book*
Emilio Villa, *The Selected Poetry of Emilio Villa*
Robert Kelly, *A Voice Full of Cities*
Pier Paolo Pasolini, *The Divine Mimesis*
Miklós Szentkuthy, *Prae, Vol. 1*
Federico Fellini, *Making a Film*

SOME FORTHCOMING TITLES

Sándor Tar, *Our Street*
Joseph Winkler, *The Graveyard of Bitter Oranges*
Ferit Edgü, *No One*

ABOUT THE TRANSLATOR

Genese Grill is a writer, artist, and German scholar living in Burlington, Vermont. She is the author of *The World as Metaphor in Robert Musil's The Man without Qualities: Possibility as Reality* (Camden House, 2012) and the American representative of The International Robert Musil Society.

Lightning Source UK Ltd.
Milton Keynes UK
UKHW021304120223
416889UK00021B/750